WILFUL HEIRESS

h Silverwood is young,
an heiress, but no fool.
nces of a notorious rake,
pursued and her carriage
A personable young farmer
proves to be much more to
Sir Maurice. Unfortunately
pises everything she stands
he helps her straighten out
sehold affairs, he will not
she desires. Meanwhile Sir
his chance to revenge
, and possess himself of the

THE WILFUL HEIRESS

The Wilful Heiress

by

Veronica Heley
writing as Victoria Thorne

Dales Large Print Books
Long Preston, North Yorkshire,
BD23 4ND, England.

British Library Cataloguing in Publication Data.

Heley, Veronica writing as Thorne, Victoria
   The wilful heiress.

   A catalogue record of this book is
   available from the British Library

   ISBN   978-1-84262-589-7 pbk

First published in Great Britain in 1985 by Robert Hale Limited

Copyright © Victoria Thorne 1985

Cover illustration © Len Thurston by arrangement with
P.W.A. International Ltd.

The moral right of the author has been asserted

Published in Large Print 2008 by arrangement with
Victoria Thorne, care of Watson, Little Ltd.

Dales Large Print is an imprint of Library Magna Books Ltd.

Printed and bound in Great Britain by
T.J. (International) Ltd., Cornwall, PL28 8RW

ONE

'I may be an heiress, but I am not a fool!' The Lady Elisabeth Silverwood frowned at her aunt. 'Sir Maurice Winton is an evil man, and I'll hear no more of him and his love for me. Indeed I suspect that he loves my moneybags more than he loves me.'

'Oh, my dear!' Mrs Marriott raised mittened hands in protest. 'I'm sure Sir Maurice is devoted to you. He's told me so a dozen times. And the way he looks at you...'

'As if he owns me already,' said Elisabeth, with a shudder. 'I know how he looks at me, and I don't like it. The man is...'

'A gentleman,' said her aunt.

'As far as blood goes, yes. But he spills other people's blood far too readily for my liking.'

'Surely it's something of a compliment to have men fight over you, my love?'

'Not when they kill one another.'

The coach lurched onwards, raising dust from the country road. They had left the smooth turnpike some while ago, and were making slow progress through the wooded hills and valleys of the Warwickshire countryside.

Elizabeth's maid sat in the opposite corner of the coach to her mistress, clutching the jewel case.

Elisabeth's aunt was a faded, complaining blonde of some forty summers. She knew all the ins and outs of Society, but she did not know how to control her headstrong niece. A distant relative, she had been left badly off when her husband died, and had been pleased at first to take charge of a girl who was young, and doubly an heiress. But there were drawbacks, and this journey, undertaken in haste and in secret, was one of them.

'If you wished to avoid Sir Maurice,' said Mrs Marriott, 'then why couldn't we have gone to Bath, or Tunbridge Wells? There is plenty of good society there.'

'I am tired of Society,' said Elisabeth, with a yawn. She pulled at the glossy lovelock that lay over her shoulder. Her hair was dark, and free of powder. If she had worn sackcloth, it would have become all the rage but today she was ultra fashionable in a panniered gown of blue silk. The low-cut bodice was trimmed with rich lace, and there were more falls of lace about her elbows. A diamond pin sparkled in her piled-up hair, and there was a necklet of pearls about her pretty neck. She made a charming picture, and yet she did not look happy.

She said, 'I thought we'd have arrived before now.'

8

'I'm in no haste to arrive,' said her aunt. 'From what I remember of Denys Hall the chimneys smoke, and none of the beds will be aired.'

'We can set all that to rights. I'm fond of the place, and I'd have bought it outright if I could. While my dear guardian was alive, it was the nearest thing I had to a home of my own.'

'The man was rude to me, the last time we came. I doubt if anyone but you, Elisabeth, grieves for his death.'

'Yes, I know he quarrelled with everyone around him, but he was always good to me, and I miss him.' There was a sheen of tears in Elisabeth's eyes.

'A most difficult man,' declared Mrs Marriott. 'I shall never understand why your father appointed Sir William as your guardian.'

'Perhaps because he was rich,' said Elisabeth, with a trace of cynicism. 'For after all, he has left me all his money … and added to what father left me…' She sighed. 'But it was more likely that father knew we liked one another. He was a lonely man, and I wish I'd seen more of him.'

'If he was so fond of you, then why didn't he leave you the Hall as well as all his money?'

'He couldn't. The estate was entailed on a distant relation. The new owner won't sell, but as he can't afford to live there himself, he's agreed to rent me the house and estate on a long lease. At last I shall have a home of my own in the country.'

'You have other houses...'

'But none that I like so well. Don't look so miserable, aunt. I daresay I'll grow tired of the country as quickly as I grow tired of everything else. And then we will move on to Paris, or Rome ... or to the devil.'

'I daresay Sir Maurice may have something to say about that.'

'Aunt, I forbid you to mention him again. I detest the man, and there's an end to it.'

'It takes two,' said her aunt, with a smirk. 'You may have thought you'd put him off the scent by saying we were bound for relatives in the Lake District, but I saw him in close conversation with one of your footmen yesterday, and I doubt if they were discussing the weather.'

'You mean he may have bribed my servant to tell him where we were going?'

'Why not? All's fair in love and war. In the country Sir Maurice will have a clear field, unencumbered by all your other suitors...'

'Never!' declared Elisabeth. But she was uneasy. She thrust her head out of the window, and called up to her coachman to go faster.

The coach was grinding up a long drag of a hill, and the horses had slowed to a walk.

Behind them the road dropped away into a valley, and another coach could now be seen following them, trailing a cloud of dust.

The coach occupied by Lady Elisabeth, her aunt and her maid, was a large, cumbersome affair, drawn by four horses. It was piled high with luggage, and a footman was seated up on top beside the coachman; both men were armed with guns against highwaymen and beggars. A postboy also rode with them; he had been supplied by the last coaching inn, where they had changed horses. All this meant that the Lady Elisabeth travelled in state, but it also meant that she did not travel fast.

The coach following them was a much lighter affair, with no luggage on top, and only a coachman to drive it. It was drawn by two horses, only these were no lumbering posthorses, but a matched pair, black as night; a familiar sight in London.

Elisabeth felt a tremor of fear touch her, as she tried to pick out the coat-of-arms painted on the side doors of the following coach. Her aunt took a pair of folding glasses from her pocket, and focussed them out of the other window.

'My dear, is it Sir Maurice? Has he caught up with us already? Well, I declare he is no laggard in love. Yes, I am almost sure it is his chaise.'

Elisabeth sank back into her corner of the

coach. Something very like a sob of fear rose in her throat, and her hands quivered as they pulled her cloak more closely about her neck.

Only the previous evening Sir Maurice had bent over her chair, and let his long white hands linger on her neck. She had pulled away, trying not to let him see how much his presence disturbed her, but those dark eyes of his had noticed the movement, and he had smiled. He had large white teeth which snapped together when he was displeased. He was a smooth-faced man, with a lightweight voice and an air of violence about him. He wore beautiful clothes, and his wig was more elaborate than most.

When she had first met him, Elisabeth had been intrigued. He had a bad reputation, having already killed three men in duels. He was known to be on the lookout for an heiress, since his fortune was small, and his tastes expensive. All this merely amused Elisabeth, who was accustomed to being pursued by indigent young gentlemen. Sir Maurice was not so young, and he was not deterred by her cool behaviour towards him.

When she rode in the Park, he came to her side, riding one of his famous black horses. If she attended a rout party, he would somehow contrive to become her partner. If she danced, he would hover at the side of the ballroom, watching her, and sending meaning glances at any other gentleman who dared to stand up with her.

The gossips began to say Sir Maurice would tame the lovely Elisabeth by the end of the Season. There was no one to protect her save her aunt, who seemed to admire Sir Maurice.

Elisabeth's mother had died when the child was young, whereupon her father had placed his only child in a select boarding school at Bath. There she spent all her childhood and youth, except when she was allowed to visit her guardian at Denys Hall for a few weeks every summer. Elisabeth's father had never liked England, and after a while he sold his country home and lived abroad.

At eighteen Elisabeth was an orphan, mistress of a palazzo in Rome, an apartment in Paris, a town house in London, and a fortune in gilt-edged stocks.

Her guardian had rarely come to London, but he found a distant cousin to act as chaperone to Elisabeth, and she plunged into the limelight of Society. It was only natural that her head should have been turned. She was young, beautiful, and rich. Men flocked around her, and she became the Toast of the Town. Elisabeth enjoyed every minute of her first season, from her presentation at Court to the Masquerades. In the autumn she had gone abroad with her aunt, to take up much the same sort of life in Rome and Paris.

Her guardian had advised her to take her time in choosing a husband, and since she was financially independent, she had done so. Now and then she met a man she liked, but never a one did she like enough to marry.

By her fourth season she had begun to feel jaded. The round of parties, of dressing and undressing, of compliments and over-heated rooms ... all wearied her.

Then into her circle came a young man fresh from the country, and he was good to look at. Henry Dart was not particularly wealthy, nor was he particularly well-born, but he had clear grey eyes and square shoulders, and he seemed to mean it when he told her that he loved her.

She didn't mean to marry him, of course; he was too young, too callow for that. She thought he would make a faithful husband, but that if she married him, she would be bored within a week.

Yet she did not send him away, and when Sir Maurice cast sidelong glances at young Henry, she smiled.

It never occurred to her that Sir Maurice would kill the lad. Why should it? She did not mean to marry Henry Dart.

One evening Sir Maurice picked a quarrel with Henry over a card game, and two days later the lad's eyes gazed lifelessly up at the leaves of a tree in a secluded corner of Regent's Park.

That night Sir Maurice appeared at Elisabeth's side as usual. She looked in vain for Society to condemn him, but according to Society, Sir Maurice had acted correctly. He had so contrived matters that the young man had struck the first blow and issued the challenge to the duel. There had been seconds appointed in the usual manner, a doctor had been in attendance. All had been done according to Society's rules.

Only Elisabeth, it appeared, was shocked. And she was shocked.

She was filled with remorse, and anger, and fear. She felt that she had killed Henry Dart as surely as if she had run him through the heart herself. She left the party early, and the next day she sent for her man of business.

Mr Deeds had conducted the business affairs of her father, and of her guardian, Sir William Denys. For some months now, ever since the death of her guardian, she had been negotiating the lease of Denys Hall and the surrounding estate. Now she declared that she would wait no longer. Mr Deeds must so arrange matters that she could move in at the end of that week. She would continue to pay the wages of such servants as remained there, and would engage new ones when she arrived. But all must be made ready in haste, and in secret. She did not wish Sir Maurice to learn of her plans.

With all her heart she longed to withdraw from Society, to recover her shaken nerve.

And now Sir Maurice was hunting her down like the crafty fox that he was.

Elisabeth shivered as she sat in the corner of her coach. Almost she could feel his hot breath on her neck again, and the slither of his fingers over her skin.

But no! She would not give in without a fight.

She leaned out of the window again, urging the coachman to greater speed. They were nearly at the top of the hill. In a moment they would begin the descent into another valley, cross the river at the bottom by the ancient ford, and then would enter the network of narrow lanes which criss-crossed the Denys estate.

Once they were across the ford and into those tiny lanes, nothing could pass their coach, and she would be safe.

They were breasting the rise. In a moment the horses would be able to pick up speed, and then...

She glanced back down the hill in a frenzy. She could pick out the coat of arms on the door of the pursuing coach clearly, and she recognised it for that of Sir Maurice. He was gaining on them.

She told herself not to be a fool. What

could he do, if he were indeed to catch them up? He could not abduct her, surely! Did she not have her coachman, and her footman and an outrider to guard her? Not to mention her aunt and her maid.

But somehow she was not reassured. Her dread of Sir Maurice might or might not be justified, but she would very much rather not put the matter to the test.

There was another traveller on this road today, going in the opposite direction. At the top of the hill a single horseman had dismounted to adjust his saddlebags and to look back over the beautiful valley he had just left.

As Elisabeth's coach passed the horseman she had ample time to notice how well the fawn-coloured broadcloth sat over his shoulders. He was a gentleman, undoubtedly. Not only did he wear a sword, but in every trifling detail of his appearance, there was good breeding. There was nothing flashy about his clothes, and they were not new, but everything was in good taste. He did not wear a wig, but like men she had seen of advanced, liberal views, he had powdered his hair and tied it back with a ribbon.

He had fine grey eyes, and a square chin to match square shoulders.

He reminded Elisabeth, for a poignant moment, of Henry Dart, but this man was taller, and older, and looked as if anything he undertook to do, would be carried out with energy and efficiency.

As Elisabeth looked at the stranger, first with mild curiosity, and then with interest, so he returned the look. He glanced at the coat of arms on the door of her coach and frowned. He gave a quick lift of his shoulders and turned his head, taking a step in her direction as if intending to speak to her.

Did she know him?

No, surely not. She would have remembered if she had ever met anyone with such piercing grey eyes and such a handsome profile in London. Why, he would have stood out like a gold ring in a tray of brass farthings!

Her chaise began to gather speed as they dropped down the hill. Elisabeth glanced back. Sir Maurice's coach was coming into sight, and the stranger was remounting his horse.

They were approaching the ford. Would they get across in time? She was in a fever, biting her lip ... her aunt screamed that they were going too fast, and would surely overturn...

They had reached the bottom of the hill, and were splashing into the ford, but now Sir Maurice's chaise was drawing level, and thrusting them off course.

There was a grinding crash, and the coach halted, tilting at an ominous angle.

Elisabeth was thrown to her knees. Mrs Marriott became entangled with the maid, and both continued to scream.

The upper door open, and Sir Maurice's dark-visaged face looked in on them. He was laughing.

'What a lucky accident! The wheel of your coach is jammed over the edge of the causeway, my lady, and you must accept a seat in my carriage, if you please.'

Elisabeth felt sick with fear. Had he engineered the accident by skilfully dangerous driving? It seemed very much like it.

'Thank you,' she said, struggling upright. 'But I am sure that will not be necessary. If we leave the coach ourselves, and take the luggage off the roof, then I'm sure my people will be able to right it.'

'You'll need a team of oxen to drag your coach to safety, my dear. Send one of your fellows on to the nearest inn, to fetch them. Your aunt and your maid can await them here, and I'll take you on to your destination in my chaise.'

Mrs Marriott was clutching at Elisabeth's dress.

'I'm sure we're sinking! Elisabeth, are we going to drown?'

'No, of course not! Where are your smelling salts, aunt? Use them! Sir Maurice, if you will assist my aunt and my maid into your chaise...'

'There is no room for them, my dear. As you'll see, my valet occupies the whole of the front seat, together with my luggage. There is only room for you.'

'Never!'

Elisabeth struggled with the door beside her, and succeeded in getting it open at last, even though it was partly under water. Her satin shoes with their diamond buckles were soaked through, and so was the hem of her dress. The river was running dangerously high and fast. Could she wade through it to the bank, without being swept off her feet?

She called out to the coachman and footman to help her, but they were busy with the horses, trying to cut them free.

There was a swish of water, and the stranger from the top of the hill came into view, riding his fine bay mare. He doffed his tricorne hat. He did not smile, and his manner was cool.

'Might I be of assistance, ma'am? I fear it'll be some time before your coach will be able to continue the journey. May I assist you to the bank?'

'Who the devil are you?' That was Sir Maurice.

The stranger looked at Elisabeth as if expecting her to provide Sir Maurice with his name.

Then he said, 'Robin Prior, gentleman farmer, at your service.'

'Elisabeth!' A shriek from Mrs Marriott. 'The coach is sinking!'

Elisabeth clung to the strap at the side of the window. It was true that the coach seemed to be slipping further into the river.

'I thank you, sir,' said Elisabeth to the stranger. 'If you'll assist me to the bank, then...'

'Then I will drive you to the Hall,' Sir Maurice called up to his coachman to be ready to drive on and up out of the ford.

'No!' cried Elisabeth. 'I do not wish to be alone with that man!'

'Then I will take you across country to the Hall myself,' said Robin Prior. 'If you will trust yourself to me.'

'What of my aunt?'

'Your servants will be able to assist her to dry land, and I don't think the coach will tilt any further.'

'Very well, I accept your offer.'

She was amazed at herself for allowing a perfect stranger to pluck her from the coach, and she was a little frightened at what Sir Maurice might do when he caught up with her ... but in the meantime...

In the meantime, Robin Prior's arms were strong, and from the first moment that he touched her, she knew that she would be safe with him. She was tucked into the crook of his arm, with her head resting against his shoulder, before Sir Maurice realised what was happening. Robin urged his horse to pick her way out of the river while Sir Maurice was still cursing at his coachman to hurry.

'After them!' cried Sir Maurice.

Robin Prior smiled, grimly. He pricked his horse to a trot, and after following the road for some twenty yards, turned off it into a bridle path leading deep into the woods. Sir Maurice and his chaise would not be able to follow them there.

The last glimpse Elisabeth had of the ford, showed her the servants wading back to help Mrs Marriott and the maid from the coach. Then the trees closed in about them, and all was silent.

'Am I awake or dreaming?' she said.

TWO

'Quiet!' said the stranger.

Elisabeth pouted. 'Sir you are not very gallant!' Did he not know how he ought to respond when rescuing a beautiful damsel in distress?

'I'm listening for sounds of pursuit.' He gave Elisabeth a quelling look.

'Oh, they can't follow us through these woods, I'm sure. Heyday, what a lovely evening it's going to be!'

Still he did not take the hint, but reined in his horse at a junction where two paths met.

'Can you direct me?' he said. 'And leave the chatter till we are safe at the Hall? Ought we to take the right fork – or the left?'

She sat up, and looked about her.

'The right fork takes us to the edge of the Park, and from there you...'

'I know my way from there.'

She lay back in his arms, and lowered her lashes so that she could study his face. She decided that he was indeed one of the handsomest men she had ever seen, but that his features would be improved by a more pleasant expression. He did not look as if he were enjoying this adventure as he ought.

Since he did not seem to wish to talk, she could amuse herself by observing him, and trying to guess from what walk of life he might come. If his clothes had been made for him by a country tailor, then he had spent his money well, but there was only the bare minimum of lace on his shirt of softest lawn.

It looked to her as if he appreciated quality, but despised high fashion, for there was neither braid nor lace, nor even gold buttons on his coat, and his pockets showed evidence of use, which no gentleman aspiring to fashion, would ever permit.

Elisabeth began to wish that he would turn that firm chin of his down, and show some sign that he was holding a lovely young woman in his arms, instead of a bale of washing. She sighed, and glanced upwards through her lashes at him.

'Are you tired? It's not far now,' he said.

'I am a little tired,' she said. Was the man made of iron? She had never before met a man who showed so little awareness of her person.

She stirred in his arms, and pulled her lovelock forward, to lie more prettily over her shoulder.

'Tell me,' she said in a coaxing voice, 'To whom I am indebted for rescuing me?'

'I thought I had told you. My name is Robin Prior. I had some business to attend to hereabouts, and was making my way back home across country when I observed that your coach had met with an accident. Naturally I offered my assistance; and here we are entering the Home Park.'

Elisabeth sighed, for the ride would soon be over, and the stranger intrigued her.

'You are well acquainted with this part of the world, for a stranger,' she said.

'I spent a summer holiday hereabouts some years ago, and rode about the place as boys will. To anticipate your next question, it is the talk of the countryside that the Lady Elisabeth Silverwood is expected to take up residence at Denys Hall today. And here is the gate into the paddock, at last.' He sounded thankful.

She was piqued. 'You seem anxious to be rid of me, sir.'

'I have no small talk. I fear you find me dull.'

Now she was amused. 'There are worse things in life than a lack of small talk.' And here she thought of Sir Maurice.

'So,' he said, in measured tones. 'You do find me dull? I suspected as much.'

'Oh, what an absurd creature you are! If I could find my fan, I would rap you across the knuckles with it!'

'I fear,' said Robin, his chin higher than ever, 'that I am not accustomed to move in polite society, and I would not know how to react if you attacked me with your fan.'

She gave an angry little laugh. 'There is no need to explain that you are not accustomed to Society, for it is written all over you! No doubt you were brought up in a farmyard, and went to school in a barn!'

His mouth became compressed with anger, but he let no word escape him.

By now she was filled with the desire to strike some spark from him. One moment she wanted to box his ears, and the next she wanted to put her arms up about his neck, and pull his head down, so that he could...

What? Did she really wish this stuck-up, Puritan of a farmer to kiss her?

She felt her face flood with colour, and for the first time was glad that he was still obstinately looking over her head.

He bent down to release the catch on the gate which led into the stable yard, but it was rusty with disuse. He dismounted, leaving her in the saddle. He wrenched the gate open with a heave of powerful shoulders, led her through into the middle of the cobbled yard, and hallooed for a groom.

The place was deserted. The loose boxes were all empty, and weeds grew between the cobblestones.

Elisabeth loved this old place. Denys Hall was a rambling old house built partly of stone taken from the ruins of an ancient abbey which had once flourished there, and partly of rose-red brick. It had been altered many times in its chequered history, so that no one style predominated.

'We should have gone round to the front,' she said, sliding down onto the mounting block, and shaking out her skirts.

'But we approached from the rear,' he said. He looked around, frowning. 'This place has been disgracefully neglected, and it will need a lot of money spent on it. Look at the missing tiles...'

'You have no soul. See how pretty the dovecote looks, high up on the stable roof, with the elms rising behind...'

'I have no taste for the picturesque,' said Robin, 'if it is brought about by poor husbandry. Missing tiles mean leaking roofs, and leaking roofs mean trouble!'

He tied his mare to a ring set in the wall nearby, with the rapid efficiency that seemed second nature to him.

'What an adventure this is!' declared Elisabeth. 'The heroine arrives in the deserted house ... no, let us make it an enchanted palace...'

Robin looked down his nose at her. 'I have no taste for romantic literature, and the only enchantment around here was brought about by Sir William Deny's parsimony. He can't have spent a penny on the estate for years!'

He led the way to the back door. It was

stuck fast in its frame. Robin set his shoulder to the door, and threw it open.

He seemed to know the way through the back quarters of the house. Elisabeth followed where he led. She was a little subdued by the signs of neglect about her. The hall seemed cocooned in cobwebs, and puffs of dust arose about her feet. She lifted her skirts above her ankles, and noticed that there were several sets of tracks in the dust before her.

A quavering voice hailed them. 'Who's there? Is that you, my lad?'

'No,' said Robin Prior, short and sharp. 'It is Lady Elisabeth.'

A short, bewigged personage in black came into view. Elisabeth gave a little scream of recognition, and rushed past Robin to greet him.

'Oh, Mr Deeds! I am so glad to see you here! Our coach was upset at the ford, and this gentleman kindly carried me here, but there are no servants, it seems … and my maid and my aunt are still on their way here. What an adventure!'

Mr Deeds mopped his brow. 'My lady, I fear you have every right to be angry, but there is nothing prepared for you here, as you can see. I sent orders to Sir William's old butler to hire servants, and have the place ready against your coming, but it appears that the old man died a month ago, and nothing has been done. I have sent my clerk into the village – I thought it was him returning when I heard your footsteps – but he has not yet returned with any servants, and I myself must press on to reach Warwick tonight.'

Elisabeth looked at the cheerless, dirty hall, and said, 'Then what is to be done?'

Robin knew. 'You must put up at the inn in the village nearby until such time as this place can be made habitable.'

Elisabeth turned her shoulder on him. It was a reasonable suggestion, but because it had come from him, she had no wish to adopt it. She said, 'You yourself could ride to the village for me now, to hurry up the servants and bespeak a meal. I have no taste for sleeping in inns, when my own house lies empty.'

'But, my lady...' That was Mr Deeds, glancing from one to the other.

'Very well,' said Robin, with a thunderous look at Mr Deeds. 'I will see you safely bestowed in one of the better rooms, have a word with Mr Deeds, and be off.'

'No, no!' declared Mr Deeds, mopping his brow again. 'You must not...'

'An excellent idea,' declared Elisabeth. She swept to the nearest door, and waited for Robin to open it for her. He came to himself with a start, and hastened to throw the double doors wide for her to pass through. She went into the library, and he closed the doors after her.

She looked about her with interest. This had been her guardian's favourite room, and therefore was less neglected than the rest. She ran her fingers along the edge of a large leather chair, grimaced, and automatically looked around for the bell-rope, to summon a maid with a duster. But of course there was at the moment no maid in the house for her to summon. She decided that she would turn housewife, and dust the chair herself.

She pulled open the double doors and stopped short, for Mr Deeds and Robin Prior were having a low-voiced but heated argument by the front door.

Mr Deeds was saying, '…No, no! It is not right that you should be…'

'Mr Deeds, I cannot leave her here alone to…'

Both men glanced up, and caught sight of her.

'Yes, my lady?' said Robin, sending Mr Deeds another of his frowning glances.

'I was looking for something to clean the chair with,' said Elisabeth, feeling foolish. 'But I fear I interrupted you.'

'Not at all,' said Robin. 'I am about to leave for the village. I should be back within the hour. Mr Deeds will stay here until…'

'I greatly regret,' said Mr Deeds, taking out a turnip watch, and consulting it with a feverish air. 'I am in court tomorrow in Warwick, and must therefore be on my way…'

Elisabeth said, 'It is clear that Mr Deeds should rout out his clerk and some servants in the village, on his way back to Warwick. I am sure Mr Prior will keep me company until such time as…'

Mr Deeds pressed his fingers to his brow. 'But, my lady! It is true that I am in haste, but this gentleman…' He glanced at Robin. 'It is not seemly that he … that Mr … er…'

'Prior,' said Robin.

'It is not seemly that he stay here.'

'Why not?' said Robin, raising one eyebrow. 'Mr Deeds, the longer you delay, the longer my lady will be without heat, light or food.'

Elisabeth extended her hand to Mr Deeds. 'Thank you for your kind thoughts, but indeed Mr Prior is right, and if he offers to stay with me, then I will be glad of his company.'

Mr Deeds kissed her hand, got as far as the front door, and came back to say that he had forgotten to tell Elisabeth that the keys to the house, and the inventory of its contents were on the hall chest. Robin held the front door open, assisted Mr Deeds to mount the horse he had left tied to a ring outside the front door, and waved him goodbye.

Alone in the hall for a moment, Elisabeth saw that there were many more tracks in the dust, going to and from different rooms and up the stairs. Also, there were three glasses and a half-empty bottle of wine on a side-table. The glasses looked as if someone had only just used them.

She pointed these things out to Robin. 'Do you think we have been burgled?'

'No, no. It will have been Mr Deeds and his clerks, checking the inventory, I suppose, while he awaited your arrival.'

Mr Deeds had only spoken of one clerk, and not two. Elisabeth opened her mouth to remind Robin of this, but he was on his way back into the library, saying that he would try to light a fire there for her.

'Do you know how?' she asked.

'I have watched the maids at it often enough.'

He stripped off his close-fitting buff coat, and laid it on the great leather chair before the fire, so that Elisabeth could sit down in safety.

His fawn waistcoat fitted him without a wrinkle, and his shoulders looked even broader without the coat. Fashionable gentlemen sported much embroidery on their waistcoats, but Robin Prior had been satisfied with an edging of brown silk twist. Elisabeth decided that Robin's decision to flout fashion must be a matter of choice, and not of poverty, for the material of which the waistcoat was made had been cut from an expensive watered silk, and his buckskin breeches, silk stockings and brown boots were all of the first quality.

By the time he had cleared the grate, laid a fire, and coaxed it into life, Elisabeth was thinking that she did not wish this unusual young man to vanish as soon as her aunt and the servants arrived. She wondered if she could perhaps persuade him to dance attendance on her for a few days.

There was a confused murmur in the hall. Robin investigated, and came back shortly to report that Mr Deeds' clerk appeared to have found some servants in the village, and that they were even now hard at work, preparing the main rooms, and cooking a meal.

'Oh, I'm ravenous!' cried Elisabeth. 'It's hours since we ate!'

'I've some bread and cheese in my saddlebags.'

'You are an angel in disguise!' Elisabeth clapped her hands in delight.

For the first time the stranger laughed, and a warm colour tinged the even brown of his cheeks. 'Hardly that,' he said, but brought her his saddle bags, and laid a neat packet of bread and cheese on a clean handkerchief for her to eat.

She divided the food into two, and pressed one portion on him. He ordered a serving maid to find two clean glasses, and they filled up from the half-empty bottle left in the hall.

'Oh, this is good,' said Elisabeth, stretching hands and feet to the now glowing fire.

'I fear your shoes are ruined,' he said, suddenly going down on one knee before her. He removed her satin shoes, and chafed her stockinged feet.

Elisabeth found his attentions delightful. Her light shoes had long since dried out after their immersion in the water, and she had forgotten all about wet feet. But it was undeniably pleasant to have such a stiff-necked young man kneeling before her.

From this angle his mouth, which had seemed to her rather too hard for beauty, became softened, contradicting to some extent the cutting line of his jaw.

She lowered her eyelashes. 'I fear I'm keeping you from your wife.'

'I'm not married. Would you care to remove your stockings, if I turn my back? Or shall I send for one of the village girls to maid you?'

'My stockings are dry enough. But will not your mother and sisters be sitting in the window, waiting for your return?'

'I have neither brothers nor sisters, and my mother died a year ago. Won't you take a chill if you don't remove your stockings?'

He was holding her feet as if they were made of spun glass. Elisabeth leaned back in her chair.

'You think my feet are pretty?'

'They are exquisite,' he said, in a quiet, but intense tone. Then he seemed to recollect who and what he was for he dropped her feet, and stood up in one abrupt movement. He took out a gold repeater watch.

'Your aunt and your maid should be here soon,' he said, with a return to his normal, chilly manner. 'No doubt you'll be glad to see them.'

'I shan't be glad if you treat me like a stranger.'

'You forget that I'm a mere farmer, and therefore...'

'You are also a gentleman, who has rescued me from a difficult situation.'

'You should not have put yourself into such a situation in the first place. What on earth were you doing, travelling about the countryside without the protection of some competent man?'

She began to get angry. 'If it is any business of yours – which it is not – I left Town in a hurry, and my steward, who normally arranges all travel details for me, is somewhat elderly, and anyway he is laid up at present with an ague.'

'It is all of a piece. You fine Society ladies have no consideration for others. You send for Mr Deeds at a day's notice, and demand that he put himself out to travel into the country for you...'

'He is paid for it!'

'You think you can ride rough-shod over...'

'Enough! I'll hear no more!'

'You'll hear this – and then I'll leave you...'

'Leave this instant!' She pointed to the door. 'Out!'

He bowed, formally. 'Madam, I am your obedient servant. I'll leave this house the moment your aunt and maid arrive, but not one moment sooner. Since you have been so foolish as to travel unprotected, I must necessarily stay in the house until such time as...'

She stood up, gathered his coat from beneath her, and flung it at him. 'Take that, and get out of my sight!'

He shook out his coat and donned it in furious, thin-lipped silence. Then he made his way to the door.

'Stay!' she cried. 'You have behaved very badly, but I suppose that you have been brought up to believe the worst of Society ladies...'

He inclined his head in a slight bow, but did not reply.

She bit her lip. 'Tell me why you are so angry with me? I have done you no harm that I know of ... save to delay you on your return home for a couple of hours.'

'It is what you are, what you represent.' He

glanced at the door, as if wishing himself the other side of it.

'You are angry with me because I wear silks and laces, and fine jewels?'

'No. At least ... yes, perhaps.' He sighed. 'Forgive me, if I became somewhat heated. I daresay it is not your fault that you have been taught to please yourself in everything ... to wear fine jewels while your tenants starve in homespun ... to move at a moment's notice from one splendid house to another, while in the village they plaster their walls with dung to keep out the wind...'

She did not understand him. 'But I have no tenants who ... ah, you are talking about the poor people on this estate? But what is that to me?'

He gave her a keen look. 'You are now their landlord, Lady Elisabeth. How can you say it is nothing to you?'

'But...' She made a gesture of frustration. 'All such things will be dealt with by my steward, I suppose. If there is any great hardship here then I suppose that in due course he will be looking into the matter.'

'You told me that he was not only elderly, but also laid up with an ague. In the meantime your tenants starve. Naturally,' he said, with heavy sarcasm, 'that is none of your business. You will no doubt order another silk dress or cloak lined with fur, while your steward considers the problem of leaky roofs and children who die in infancy. To pay for your new clothes you will need more money, and therefore you will order your steward – when he is recovered from his ague – to increase the rents you charge hereabouts ... and I believe the people here are already at their wits' end how to meet the last increase in rents which Sir William put upon them. But oh, no!' he said, with a curl of his lip. 'It is no business of yours!'

He had made her feel uncomfortable, but she was not going to admit it. 'Well, it is not my business, exactly. It's true that I've just signed a lease for the place, but...'

'But naturally you had no intention of bettering the lot of those who live on the estate. You need say no more! You are no better than the rest of your kind.'

'If things are really as bad as you say ... and I don't believe they can be ... but if they are, well ... I shall certainly look into it.'

'With your elderly steward laid up of an ague?'

'Well, I might employ some other man, perhaps, just for this estate. Some bailiff...'

'...who will, I daresay, line his own pockets, while fleecing you and your tenants. And you none the wiser.'

She could have struck him. 'Why, you are, without exception, the rudest, most intolerant young man I have ever met! You know nothing of me, and yet you would put all your prejudices, and your spitefulness...'

'That's not true!'

'It's very true! You leap at my throat before we are fairly introduced. If you go around hurling accusations at everyone like this, then I am sure you must be the most un-popular man in the County!'

He bowed again, stiffly. 'I will not bandy words with you, when it is obvious that you have lost your temper.'

'Lost my temper?' She beat at the panniers of her dress, and looked around for something to throw at him. There seemed to be nothing appropriate to hand. Then she had an idea, a very pleasing idea.

She said, 'If you are so concerned for the lot of my poor tenants, I challenge you to do something about it. I challenge you to take on the position of Steward to the Denys estate!'

THREE

He took a step back. 'You want me to...?' He pointed to himself, doubting that he had heard correctly.

'Yes, you.' She smiled, beginning to enjoy herself. 'Why should you not work for me, if you are so worried about my poor people?'

'But...' He looked about him with a dazed air. 'But I have my own farm, my own responsibilities...'

'I am sure you must employ a competent bailiff. You would not otherwise be racketing about the countryside, interfering in other people's business.'

'It's true that I'm well served at home, but...'

'Well, then? You will be my Steward?'

He shook his head to clear it. 'Never, madam,' he said, with an icy hauteur that transformed him into a stranger once again. 'It is quite out of the question.'

'I see, you are just another hypocrite. You care nothing for my poor people, really.' She bestowed a malicious smile on him.

His brows flattened, and he set his chin at her. 'You don't know what you're asking. And now, if you'll give me leave to depart, I must see what progress has been made here in the house, and then make my way to the inn.'

He glanced out of the window, at the darkening sky. 'I fear I'll not get any further than the village tonight.'

If she was disappointed, she did not show it. Instead, she turned her shoulder on him. In a moment she heard the doors open and then close behind him.

Her shoulders drooped. She was, she realised, rather tired. It had been a long, eventful day, and she was uneasily conscious that there was a grain of truth in what he had said. She never listened to Mr Deeds when he talked business, but she did seem to remember his saying something about the tenants … that Sir William had bled the estate to leave everything away from his heir…

She straightened her shoulders. Well, if Mr Deeds were so concerned about her tenants, he could find someone to look after them for her.

Her eyes fell on Robin's saddlebags, which were lying where he had left them. She considered summoning a maid – there must be several in the house by now, to judge by the sounds of activity – to remove his luggage, so that he need never return to the library.

But Elisabeth did not summon the maid.

Instead, she sat on a while longer looking into the fire which he had lit, and thinking about this and that ... about a square chin, and a mouth that could be firm and resolute one moment, and the next could be as gentle as a woman's ... about long-fingered, capable brown hands ... about the set of a pair of broad shoulders...

Elisabeth jumped to her feet. Why was she sitting there, thinking about an insignificant farmer, when there was much to be done? For instance, she wanted to know which bedchambers had been prepared ... and began to feel guilty about her aunt and maid, who might still be struggling at the ford.

As she went out into the hall, so her coach drew up outside the front door, and with a wail Mrs Marriott limped into view on the arm of the lady's maid. Behind them, darkly smiling, came the unwelcome but modish figure of Sir Maurice Winton.

Elisabeth halted as if she had been struck.

For hours she had forgotten the exis-tence of Sir Maurice, and yet here he was, larger than life.

'My dear!' cried Mrs Marriott, 'Such a time as we have had! I declare that if it hadn't been for Sir Maurice, we would still be at the ford.'

'My pleasure to serve you,' murmured Sir Maurice, taking Elisabeth's hand in his, and kissing it. He held on to it longer than politeness decreed, while his eyes took their usual inventory of her neck and bosom.

Elisabeth knew that her colour had risen, and hoped he would not put it down to pleasure at the sight of him. She said, with as much coldness as she could muster, that if it hadn't been for Sir Maurice, there'd have been no 'accident' at the ford in the first place.

'Not an accident,' said Sir Maurice, exposing his large white teeth in a smile. 'Merely an incident. A trifling misadventure, which was blown up out of all proportion. I assure you, my dear, there was no need for you to run away as you did.'

'I am the best judge of that,' said Elisabeth. She put her arm about her aunt's shoulders, and led her towards the library. 'Come in here, aunt, and sit by the fire awhile.'

Out of the corner of her eye, Elisabeth noticed that there were now several mob-capped and aproned servants hovering about. The hall showed signs of strenuous cleaning and polishing. The tracks on the floor had disappeared, and there was even a fire on the hearth.

Elisabeth enquired whether there was a bedchamber yet prepared for Mrs Marriott.

'Certainly, my lady. Mr Prior suggested the Chinese room for Mrs Marriott, and he is sending a girl up with a warming pan for the bed immediately.'

'I knew the sheets would be damp!' Mrs Marriott fished out a well-used handkerchief. 'We shall all get rheumatism!'

'No, no,' said Elisabeth, soothingly. 'You will find everything in order, and a meal will be served in...' She raised an eyebrow at the servants.

'In half an hour's time, my lady, in the panelled parlour. Mr Prior said he did not feel the dining-room should be used until the ceiling had been attended to.'

'Then I'll go to my room at once,' declared Mrs Marriott. 'If you can spare one of the girls here to maid me...'

She was wafted away. Another of the maidservants took charge of Elisabeth's own maid, and she was left with Sir Maurice, who, it appeared, was none too anxious to leave.

Elisabeth said, 'I thank you for bringing my aunt here Sir Maurice, but as you will have observed, we are not yet ready to receive visitors.'

Sir Maurice refused to take the hint. He strolled to the fireplace, and stretched out his white hands to the fire.

'Who is this man Prior? Is he the butler here?'

'No. You must remember the name. He rescued me at the ford.'

'Oh. Really?' Sir Maurice appeared to be

amused. 'Well, I daresay he has many parts, even if good manners do not appear to be among them.'

In a way, Elisabeth agreed with Sir Maurice. She gritted her teeth.

At this inauspicious moment, Robin entered the hall, looking as point-device as ever. No cobweb had attached itself to him in his journeyings about the Hall, nor any smut from the fire he had lighted.

He did not appear to notice Sir Maurice, but addressed himself formally to Elisabeth.

'They are preparing the Tapestry Bedroom for you, my lady, and I have told them to take the trunks and other luggage there by the back stairs. There is a superior sort of woman among the servants who I believe you may consider appointing as housekeeper, although I fear the cook is somewhat inexperienced, and may need to be replaced. There is an ostler of sorts now out in the stables, and your coachman is taking charge there. But I would advise you to have the guttering over the dining hall attended to tomorrow.'

'The perfect butler!' drawled Sir Maurice. He took out his quizzing glass, and put it up to survey Robin from head to foot.

'He is not my butler,' said Elisabeth. 'He was merely kind enough to assist me...'

'In how many ways?' enquired Sir Maurice. Robin turned with tightened lips to glare at Sir Maurice.

'I don't think we have been introduced. My name is Prior...'

'I remember now,' said Sir Maurice. 'You claim to be both a gentleman and a farmer, although I was not aware that one could be both.'

'Your opinion is nothing to me,' said Robin, in a tone as stiff as his back. 'I merely offered my assistance to this lady...'

'Which was quite unnecessary!' said Sir Maurice, with a snap in his voice.

Once more, colour tinged Robin's brown cheeks. 'If the Lady Elisabeth shares your opinion of my conduct, then I shall be happy to apologise.'

'Oh, that is enough!' said Elisabeth, alarmed by the viciousness of the exchange between the two men. 'Sir Maurice, I'm grateful to Mr Prior for coming to my aid, both at the ford, and here at the Hall.'

'Damned officious of him!' said Sir Maurice.

'...and now, Sir Maurice, I would bid you goodnight.'

There was a moment of startled silence. Evidently Sir Maurice had not expected to be sent away so quickly. His sleepy-looking gaze became wide-eyed. He glanced from Elisabeth to Robin, and back again.

He said, 'Does this ... butler ... or farmer ... whatever ... stay on to dine with you?'

'If he wishes,' said Elisabeth.

'Certainly not!' said Robin, at the same moment.

Elisabeth said, 'It can be of no great moment to you, Mr Prior, if you dine here or at the inn, and I wish to take your advice about the repairs needed here.'

Sir Maurice said, 'Elisabeth, this fellow is an inconvenience to me. Send him away.'

Elisabeth turned on Sir Maurice. 'Be quiet! I must tell you that I have offered Mr Prior the post of Steward here, because he evidently understands what requires to be done about the estate. He did not feel able to accept the position, because he has other responsibilities, but nevertheless...'

'I accept,' said Robin.

'What was that?' said Sir Maurice.

'I accept the position of Steward,' said Robin, speaking direct to Elisabeth and once more ignoring Sir Maurice. 'On two conditions. The first is that you give me a free hand, and enough money to pull the estate round...'

Sir Maurice said, 'Now I wonder if you are a knave or a fool?'

'I agree to your first condition,' said Elisabeth. 'And the second?'

'That I find and train a suitable bailiff for you, and that when such a man is found and trained, that you release me from your service.'

'I agree to your second condition, as well.'

'Elisabeth,' said Sir Maurice, forgetting to smile. 'This is folly!'

'I don't think so,' said Elisabeth. She extended her hand to Robin.

He took her hand in both of his, but did not kiss it.

She said, 'Mr Prior, I thank you from the bottom of my heart. I know I shall be in safe hands with you. And now, let there be no more talk of your removing to the inn. Tell the servants to prepare a suitable bed-chamber here, and to lay a place for you at table.'

'Elisabeth!' Sir Maurice was becoming annoyed. 'Have you taken leave of your senses?'

'I believe I can trust Mr Prior,' said Elisabeth, looking up into Robin's face.

'Yes, you may trust me,' said Robin. With unexpected grace, he lifted her hand to his lips, and kissed her fingers. It was not the light caress currently accepted in society, but rather it was a token of homage.

Elisabeth took her hand back into her own keeping with a feeling that she had aroused deep feelings in him where she had sought merely to flirt. She felt somewhat shaken by this brush with someone outside the rules which governed society as she knew it … and yet she did not dislike the emotions Robin had aroused in her.

'Elisabeth!' Sir Maurice took a step in her direction.

'My lady desires to be alone,' said Robin. He went to the front door, and held it open for Sir Maurice to depart.

'As you can see, Sir Maurice,' said Elisabeth, 'there is no reason for you to stay. I am in good hands now, and you may return to Town tomorrow with an easy conscience.'

'Not so, by God!' swore Sir Maurice. 'I'll go to the inn and give myself the pleasure of waiting on you tomorrow.'

In the end, Robin did not dine with Elisabeth that night, for Mrs Marriott declared she was too tired to leave her chamber, and so she and her niece dined alone at a small table there, before the fire.

Elisabeth had been a little wary of imparting the news of Robin's appointment to her aunt, but in the event, Mrs Marriott seemed pleased.

'The man seems competent enough,' said Mrs Marriott, glancing around the sumptuous apartment with satisfaction. 'It was foolish of you to leave Town without ensuring that all would be in order here. However, for once fortune has favoured you. Provided that this man Prior knows his place, he will do well enough.'

'Knows his place?' Elisabeth frowned. 'He is a gentleman.'

'But a poor one, of course. It is pleasant to have those about one who have a certain amount of breeding, and as he has been trained to appreciate civilised behaviour, he will be able to impose it on the other servants.'

Elisabeth fiddled with her knife. 'He is not exactly a servant, aunt.'

'An upper servant, of course, I daresay it will be suitable to have him dine with us on occasions, as we did with our old steward ... when there was no other company.'

'I do not expect company, here in the country.'

Mrs Marriott put her head on one side. 'What of Sir Maurice, eh? He was most attentive to me, after that little upset at the ford.'

'It was more than a "little upset", aunt. He deliberately drove my coach off course.'

'He was, perhaps, carried away by the enthusiasm of the chase. You did run away, my dear.'

Elisabeth sighed, and pushed her plate away. She signed to the hovering footman to remove the dishes.

She said, 'I don't wish you to encourage Sir Maurice to call, aunt. I have other things on my mind.'

'What else could a girl have on her mind, but matrimony? It is time you were wed, my love.'

For the first time Elisabeth wondered if her aunt were right.

Elisabeth rose bright and early next morning, and donned a rose-coloured taffeta gown whose wired skirts gave a modified version of the outline fashionable in society, without the inconvenience of having to manoeuvre one's panniers through doorways.

Robin had risen before her, and she was told that he was directing workmen at their labour of repairing the various holes in the roof of the Hall.

So Elisabeth summoned the newly-appointed housekeeper, and with an agreeable sensation of virtue, made a tour of the house from attic to capacious cellar. Everywhere there was evidence of neglect, save in a few rooms on the ground floor where Sir William had passed his last years as a recluse. The key to one of the parlours was nowhere to be found ... but it was decided to send for a locksmith, rather than to break the door down.

The housekeeper told Elisabeth that after Sir William's gout had made walking difficult, his originally bad temper had become impossible; in consequence the few remaining servants had dwindled to one, and neighbours had ceased to call.

Elisabeth completed her tour with a sinking heart. There was so much that needed to be done, that she hardly knew where to start. Wind and weather had created havoc with curtains, paint and plaster through broken windows and leaking roofs. As things had been broken or chipped, they had been thrown aside, and not replaced. Most of the linen was in shreds.

It was something of a wonder that two bedchambers, the library, and one parlour were fit to live in. In the last few months of his life Sir William had lived and slept in the library, the only room in the whole house without a cracked or broken pane of glass in its windows.

Elisabeth was on the point of sending for Robin to consult with him about repairs, when the footman announced that Sir Maurice was waiting for her in the panelled parlour.

'Why did you let him in?' demanded Elisabeth. 'Did I tell you that I was receiving visitors?'

The footman looked wooden, and Elisabeth sighed. She supposed that Sir Maurice had greased the man's palm.

'Oh, very well,' she said. 'Tell my aunt to join me in the parlour as soon as possible.' Elisabeth had no intention of holding a tete a tete with Sir Maurice, if he were to continue in the high tone he had adopted the previous day. The affair at the ford still rankled.

But it seemed that Sir Maurice had changed his tactics.

He did not smile, as he took her hand, and lifted it to his lips.

He said, 'I came to beg your pardon for what happened yesterday. Your aunt told me that I'd frightened you ... which was not my intention, believe me!'

Did she believe him? She took a seat and felt for her fan, hanging from a cord about her waist.

He did not seem as boldly sure of himself as usual. His head was not carried so high today as was usual with him, and he flicked on his wide smile, only to flick it off again almost at once.

She said, 'My aunt will join us in a moment. Will you not be seated?'

He took a chair not far from her, but instead of lounging in it, he sat on the edge, leaning forward. The footman brought in some wine. Sir Maurice refused it, without taking his eyes of Elisabeth. The footman withdrew. Elisabeth decided that she really did not care for that particular footman, and would get rid of him as soon as possible.

Sir Maurice said, 'You have forgiven me? You understand how it was? I was carried away for a moment...'

'You thought to take advantage of me. Well, luckily you were prevented from doing so.'

'You'll put the incident behind you? You will forget and forgive?'

'I daresay I'll do so quickly enough when you are back in Town.'

He shifted in his chair. 'You know I can't leave you. You've drawn me after you, like a nail to a magnet. You mustn't bid me go.'

She lifted her shoulders, and then let them fall. In a way, it was not displeasing to play the game of love with such a practiced performer as Sir Maurice.

He flicked his smile on again, sensing that she wasn't going to maintain her anger towards him for long. He held out his hand, to take hers. 'So, you will forgive and forget?'

She allowed her hand to rest in his for a second, and then withdrew it. She frowned at him, and then laughed, plying her fan.

'Well, it is over, I suppose.'

'Yes, surely you have punished me enough.'

'Have I?'

'You know that you have.' There was reproach in his voice, and in his large, eloquent eyes. There was a dash of humour in his air which she found almost irresistible. She had to tug at her sense of what was right and wrong, to resist his blandishments.

'You must speak more plainly, Sir Maurice,' she said, snapping her fan closed, and then opening it, with a flirtatious movement. 'In what way have I punished you?'

'By frowning at me.' She laughed, and hid

the laugh behind her fan.

He drew his chair even closer to hers. 'You sent me from your side last night with scant courtesy ... you appointed that country bumpkin to your household...'

'Does that offend you? I see no reason why it should.'

Sir Maurice's chair was touching her skirt. 'How could it not be a punishment, when you give orders that a mere farmer should dine with you ... instead of me.'

'He did not dine with me, as it happens.' Yet her eyes fell from Sir Maurice's keen gaze, for she knew she had intended Robin to dine with her, and she had been disappointed when it had not proved possible for him to do so.

'Ah, did he not?' Sir Maurice's knee touched hers. 'Now, that is some consolation. At first I must admit I was angry when you spoke so kindly to him ... but then on reflection, I saw that you were but exercising a woman's privilege ... that you were playing with me ... to wound me ... to punish me...'

She laughed, but the laugh sounded false in her ears. Sir Maurice was sitting far too close for her liking. She rose to pull on the bell-rope.

'I wonder what is keeping my aunt,' she said. 'I planned to ride out this afternoon, in the park, but...'

'May I accompany you?'

'No. I think not.'

'You are cruel, Elisabeth; yet I thought you had agreed to forgive me.'

'Have done, Sir Maurice! I am not in the mood for flirtation.'

Yet she had been in the mood for it a moment ago, and they both knew it.

He stood, too. 'This is not flirtation, Elisabeth.' For once there was a rough note in the mellifluous voice. 'I am in earnest. It seems you have captured something more than just my fancy. It seems you have actually managed to damage my heart.' He laughed, a hard little laugh. 'I had not thought I possessed so much heart. I find it a most inconvenient organ, when it is out of order.'

'What are you saying? That you love me?' She could not, would not believe him.

He laid his hand on his heart. 'You know that I do.'

'I know nothing of the sort. You and others like you have been swearing fidelity to me ever since I came on the Marriage Market, and I believe I know how to assess your vows of love by now. They mean nothing.'

'Perhaps my vows in the past were somewhat lightweight. Perhaps I did think you could be easily wooed and won, at first. I confess it. But now...'

'You find yourself in love because I refuse you?'

'Do you refuse me?'

She was silent. She played with her fan. She wished herself elsewhere. She wished her aunt was with her. She wished ... she did not know what she wished.

Sir Maurice insinuated his arm about her waist, and still she did not resist him. She could feel his breath warm upon her bare neck.

'Elisabeth,' he whispered in her ear. 'You are the loveliest, most captivating piece of womanhood...'

'Enough!' She twisted away from him, but without violence. 'I am in no mood for dalliance.'

'I am very much in earnest, my dear.'

She bit her lip. 'Now I suppose you will go down on one knee, and swear that you'd still love me, were I a penniless nobody.'

He gave an oddly breathless laugh. 'I am tempted to do just that, my Elisabeth, for you do indeed have the strangest effect on me.'

'But it would not be true.'

'I think,' he said, weighing his words, 'that I would still be fascinated by you, if you were indeed a penniless nobody, but I do retain enough sense not to swear I would offer marriage to you under those conditions. You know perfectly well that I am all but penniless myself, and that I couldn't afford to marry a girl without a portion. At least give me credit for being honest with you.'

She liked him none the worse for that confession.

He took her hand, and carried it to his lips. For one moment she was reminded of the way Robin had pressed her fingers to his lips last night... She closed her eyes, and drew in her breath.

Sir Maurice misinterpreted her reaction.

'So ... we are agreed to wed?'

FOUR

Before she could collect herself sufficiently to answer Sir Maurice, the parlour door opened, and in swept Mrs Marriott, closely followed by Robin.

'My dear Elisabeth! Sir Maurice! Is this not a dreadful hour to call? The country, my dears! The noise of the birds! I swear I didn't sleep a wink after daybreak!'

Sir Maurice tried to retain Elisabeth's hand in his, but she drew it away with a decided movement. She was aware that Robin had noticed Sir Maurice's close proximity to her, and it made her angry because she felt that he disapproved.

Who, she asked herself, was Robin Prior, to approve or disapprove of her behaviour?

Robin said, at his most stately, 'If you are busy, my lady, I will return later.'

'No, don't go,' said Elisabeth, frowning and then smiling in quick succession. 'I wished to speak with you, anyway.'

'What now?' said Sir Maurice, flicking on his smile. He tried to catch Elisabeth's eye, but she refused to acknowledge him.

Elisabeth spoke direct to Robin. 'I wish to ride out this afternoon with you. Will you

61

hold yourself free?'

'Of course. Do you wish to see the village or one of the farms first? I fear you will not be able to see all there is to be seen in one afternoon.'

Elisabeth swallowed. Having appointed Robin to look after her affairs, she had dismissed the matter of the poverty-stricken tenants from her mind. She had merely intended to ride about the Park, to inspect the damage last winter's storms had created.

'Good lack!' murmured Sir Maurice, his smile widening even further. 'Will your butler now have you turn into your own bailiff?'

Elisabeth flushed, but Robin stood his ground.

'Naturally her ladyship wished to see the true state of affairs for herself. I will have the horses brought around at two this afternoon.'

Sir Maurice yawned. 'Tell this fellow you are engaged to ride out with me this afternoon, Elisabeth. We could explore the Park … a pretty sort of place, I thought. And tell your man to wipe his boots before he enters civilised company again. He stinks of the farmyard.'

Now this was not true. Elisabeth had been close enough to Robin to catch the faint odour of sandalwood and lavender in which his shirts had been put up. Moreover, he was not wearing riding boots today, but a pair of well-cut shoes with steel buckles.

Elisabeth said coldly, 'Mr Prior reminds me that I have duties as well as pleasures to expect from the land, and he is right to do so. I shall certainly ride out with him this afternoon.'

Sir Maurice lost some of his sleepy air. 'You employ him to manage such things for you, Elisabeth.'

Robin's profile was like a rock, and his shoulders were rigid. Elisabeth wished she had his self-control. She took a deep breath, and told herself that there was no need to become heated over such a trifle.

She said, 'Mr Prior, I believe you have been making an inspection of the roof. Will you tell me how things are?'

Robin spoke to her alone. 'There is much to be done before another winter, or the building will be like a leaky sieve.'

'Let us abandon the Hall, then,' said Mrs Marriott, with a shudder. 'I'm sure I never wanted to come here in the first place. What do you say, Sir Maurice?'

Elisabeth frowned at her aunt, and motioned to Robin to continue.

Robin said, 'I have set men to work at once on the roofs and gutter. There seems to be no glazier in the village, but I could send for one from Warwick, if you wish.'

'Do so,' said Elisabeth. 'I want this place put in good repair at once.'

'Now as to furnishings…'

'Let us throw everything away, and start afresh,' said Sir Maurice. 'Oak furniture is completely out of fashion.'

'Now you are being absurd,' said Elisabeth. She turned back to Robin. 'The furniture is well enough as it is for the moment, but some of the carpets and nearly all the curtains will have to be replaced. Perhaps you can help me to draw up a scheme, room by room. I shall enjoy doing that.'

She looked about her, feeling the first stir of the homemaker inside her. Nothing had been altered in the Hall during Sir William's life-time; the place offered a challenge, and she accepted it.

'Oh, by the way,' she said, 'there is one thing that cannot wait, and that is the state of the linen cupboard, but I have no idea what I ought to do about it.'

Sir Maurice yawned again. 'Next we will have you sitting over a darn, Elisabeth. Surely your housekeeper is the proper person to deal with such things?'

Robin said, 'I believe you should authorise the housekeeper to go into Warwick, to replenish stocks of linen and china. She will need some kind of draft on your bank, or better still, some cash…'

'Oh, Elisabeth!' cried Sir Maurice. 'The butler will be asking you to hand over your fortune into his keeping next! Tell the man to keep his greed within limits!'

Elisabeth's colour rose, but she said to Robin, 'You shall have enough money to cover everything that needs doing, and I will ride with you this afternoon. That will be all.'

Robin bowed, and withdrew.

Mrs Marriott said, 'I believe Sir Maurice is right, my dear. What do we know of this young man, pray?'

'He is a nobody, sprung from nowhere,' said Sir Maurice. 'Very suspicious. What references did he give you, my dear?'

'Why…' Elisabeth hesitated. It was quite true that she had taken Robin as her Steward on impulse. Would it not indeed be foolish to hand over large sums of money to such a man, without checking his credentials?

'He annoys me,' said Sir Maurice. 'And I fear you will come to regret employing him, Elisabeth. Why not send him packing?'

'Because … because I think he is right,' said Elisabeth, with her chin in the air. 'I do have responsibilities now that I have taken on this estate. If you, Sir Maurice, paid more attention to your own estates, and less to the gaming tables and to whispering sweet nothings into ladies' ears, then you would not be in debt, and I would be more inclined to listen to your suit!'

Sir Maurice's eyes narrowed. 'So?' he said.

Elisabeth nodded. She extended her hand to him. 'You have my leave to retire, Sir Maurice.'

Without a word he kissed her hand, and left the room.

Elisabeth learned much that afternoon. She learned that human beings could exist in conditions of such squalor as made her skin creep. She learned that whole families dined on a loaf of bread and a soup made of cabbage stalks, and greens plucked from the hedgerows. She could have observed each household from the safety of her horse's back, but she insisted on entering and inspecting every hovel and cottage in the village.

When they had finished, she took several deep breaths. She would have a bath in scented water when she returned to the Hall. She stripped off her fine leather gloves, which had become soiled with grease and soot, and threw them onto the grass verge.

Robin made as if to dismount, to retrieve the gloves, but she stopped him, saying that she would never wear them again.

'There is so much poverty because the Hall was not employing any labour. I think you will find that every maid, every gardener, and stable boy employed at the Hall, carried back some food to his or her family every night. The more people you employ at the Hall, the better off the village will be.'

'Some of them can hardly walk, let alone work!'

'You are shocked, I fear.'

'I believe you are pleased that I am shocked.'

'Perhaps. It will do you no harm.'

'Thank you.' Grimly.

Almost he smiled. 'I meant that I had enquired before we set out, whether there were any infectious diseases in the village at present. Naturally, I would have prevented your going into the houses, if there had been.'

'But you would still have gone into the houses yourself?'

'Well yes, of course.'

She felt herself to be a poor sort of person, compared to Robin. She said, 'What do you wish done in the village?'

He looked surprised. 'Indeed, I have no idea how much money you can spare for improving your property, and the village is but one small part of it. There are four farms…'

'I cannot see them all today. Do you think the farms will be as bad as the village?'

'I have no idea. Probably not. But when I rode through the estate a couple of days ago, I noticed many fields lying fallow, and some which need draining. Money put into the farms will bring you a quick profit.'

'I daresay there is not a tile out of place on

your own farm!'

He laughed. 'If there were, it would soon be replaced, and I detest the sight of neglected land, such as you have to the south here.'

'You are speaking of the marshes, I suppose. They are very pretty.'

They rode on in silence for a while. He was leading her up a cart-track to the top of a small hill, from where they could view two of her farms at once.

Elisabeth could not remember when she had last been in the open air like this, allowing the sun and the breeze to play on her skin.

As she had observed before, Robin had an excellent seat on a horse. She decided that he made a handsome picture in his fawn clothing, riding his pretty bay mare. She wondered what he was thinking about.

The sun was sinking slowly into the west, throwing great splashes of colour onto the sparse clouds in the sky. Below the land was dreaming, azure blue and misty green.

'I love this place,' said Elisabeth. She spoke quietly, as if afraid to disturb the beauty of the evening. 'I remember the first time I came here, as a child. My father lived in Italy most of the time, you know, and I was shut up in a seminary in Bath. It was like paradise to come here, and to be allowed to roam wherever I wished.'

Robin's stern mouth relaxed into a smile.

'Sir William was very good to me, you know. Everyone else was frightened of him, because he roared at them, but I really did like him. He used to sit me on his knee in the library of an afternoon, and we would turn over the pages of his books together and he'd tell me stories of his youth. He always treated me as if I were grown up. I loved him.'

'Yet you quarrelled with him in the end, I suppose, as everyone else did.'

'No, there was no quarrel. In a way, it would have been easier to understand if there had been. He seemed to like my visiting him less, as I got older. Perhaps it was the gout, which made him dislike my chatter.'

'There was no quarrel?' He seemed to find that hard to believe.

'No. Only, when I wrote asking to visit him, and he did not reply, I did not press the matter as I ought to have done. He found Mrs Marriott to chaperone me, and he told me I ought to write to him from wherever I happened to be. So I wrote once a month at first ... and then perhaps once every six weeks. But I never thought he would die so soon, or I would have come down to see him again, whether he had invited me or not.'

'Perhaps visitors were more of a trial than a pleasure at the end of his life, when he was failing.'

Tears blurred her sight, and she brushed them away. 'Everyone seems to think I'm glad that he's dead, because he left his money to me ... but I'm not. Really, I'm not.'

'I believe you.'

She gave him a tremulous smile. 'Thank you, Robin. I do grieve for him, and I do wish I could have seen him just once more. Thank you for being so understanding.'

They rode back through the twilight to the Hall, and though they did not speak again, they were in harmony with one another.

For three days Elisabeth rode about the estate with Robin, talking to farmers, inspecting housing and barns. For three days Robin rode one pace behind her, and enacted the part of her steward to perfection. If she called him by his Christian name, he would reply with a firm 'my lady' or occasionally 'ma'am.' When she tried to draw him out of his shell, he would remind her that they had much yet to see.

Had she merely imagined that moment in the library when he had held her foot in his hands, and called it 'exquisite'? And what of that moment when he had pressed her fingers to his lips, and sworn to serve her?

She frowned and pouted. He took no notice.

She smiled at him, and he turned his head away.

She was piqued. Not so did the gallants in society treat her. One moment she wished herself back in Town, surrounded by gentlemen sighing sonnets to her eyebrows, and vowing to love her till death … and the next moment she found herself singing as she rode along, because the countryside looked so lovely, and she was young and healthy and good to look at … and because Robin was the handsomest, cleverest man she had ever seen.

He seemed to know by instinct what ought to be done about the estate, even though he was not above taking advice from the men who had been farming the land for years. He was very popular with the tenants, and Elisabeth's heart swelled with pride when she saw how he was greeted with smiles everywhere he went.

Because he spent so much time on affairs of the estate, he had little to spend with her, and this she did not like. She would have liked to draw him into conversation when neighbours called at the Hall, but he steadfastly refused to enter the parlour when there were visitors, saying that he had overmuch to do.

Elisabeth had decided that she would have the panelled parlour completely refurnished, and said she would use the sunny morning parlour instead. Now this was the room which they had discovered to be

71

locked. Robin was absent on business that morning, and since the locksmith had not yet made an appearance, Elisabeth decided that they should all hunt for the missing key.

Sure enough, the key was eventually found on the lintel above the door, and the room found to be in comparatively good order. Elisabeth declared that she would sit there in future, while the panelled parlour was being refurnished. She had always liked this room. Sir William had been accustomed to sit there of a morning, too.

The maids descended on the place, and within the hour it was ready for occupation. Not a moment too soon, it appeared, for that morning the Hartleys called on Elisabeth.

The Squire and his wife had brought both their coltish sons with them this time. Elisabeth suspected that the young men had been informed that she was an heiress, because they paid her extravagant, awkward compliments and jostled for position at her side. The Squire beamed on everyone, his lady talked to Mrs Marriott about the latest fashions, and the young men breathed heavily and did not take their eyes off Elisabeth even when accepting refreshments.

Elisabeth found them pleasant, if tedious.

Sir Maurice, who had also called that morning, expressed something of her feelings when he said that a little beef and brawn went a long way.

'I suppose so,' said Elisabeth, 'But I am glad they are gone for another reason. Look!'

She pointed to the wall by the fireplace, on which hung half a dozen miniatures of the Denys family, painted at different times by different artists.

Sir Maurice put up his glass to inspect them.

'Members of your late guardian's family, I presume? Damned stiff-looking lot, ain't they?'

'Yes, but...' Elisabeth went down on her knees in a billow of silk. She ran her fingers over the wallpaper, which showed two darker oval patches where pictures had once hung. 'Can you see? It looks as though two more miniatures ought to hang here. Yes, here are the nails from which they hung. There were eight family portraits here the last time I came. I am sure of it.'

'Can you remember which ones are missing?'

Elisabeth put her fingers to her temples. 'A man in a red coat, in an elaborate frame with the Denys arms on it. I think, though I cannot be sure, that the other was a copy of one of the portraits upstairs in the Gallery.'

The housekeeper denied all knowledge of the missing miniatures. After all, said she, had the room not been locked all this time, and no-one able to enter it?

'But the key was available, to those who knew where to look,' observed Sir Maurice. 'What says your steward?'

'He has ridden out,' said Elisabeth. She met Sir Maurice's meaning glance, and her colour rose. 'Oh, he would not know anything about this. How could he?'

'Very easily, I should think,' said Sir Maurice.

'It is impossible! You cannot suspect him!'

'If he is innocent, then he has nothing to fear,' said Sir Maurice. 'Now, my dear, you know nothing of this man or his antecedents. It would be a simple matter for him to take advantage of you by abstracting certain valuables from the house.'

'I am sure he would never…'

'There was an inventory, I suppose?' said Sir Maurice.

'Why, yes. Mr Deeds left it on the hall table. I don't know what became of it after that.'

'Quite so,' said Sir Maurice, smiling.

Elisabeth laughed, snapping her fan at him. 'You are quite wrong, you know. Robin Prior is no thief. I daresay one of the servants may have removed the miniatures while they were cleaning the place this morning.'

Mrs Marriott coughed. 'My dear, I was only in this house a couple of times before Sir William became so strange, but I noticed that one of the miniatures had a valuable diamond-encrusted frame. Sir William saw me looking at it, and took it off the wall, to show me. The frame had been made for him in London specially. I believe the subject of the portrait had been someone close to him … his brother, perhaps? I can't remember. But none of the miniatures which remain are ornamented in just that way.'

'Ah-ha!' said Sir Maurice. 'Then the reason for their absence is clear. My dear,' And here he took Elisabeth's cold hand in his, 'You must not let your heart rule your head in this. This villain Prior…'

'He is no villain, I am sure of it.'

'You owe it to your position to make some enquiries about the man, at the very least.'

'I am sure he has nothing to hide.'

'If that is so, we can soon clear his name. But you must promise me one thing, Elisabeth, and that is that you will not alarm him into flight by telling him that we have noticed the loss of the miniatures.'

'I … I will think about it.'

She thought Sir Maurice intended to press the matter, but he did not. Instead he released her hand, and bade her good-day. He was indeed behaving himself very well at the moment, and Elisabeth was little by little losing her old fear of him.

When he had gone, Mrs Marriott said, 'Well, my dear; did I not tell you so?'

75

'Tell me what, aunt?'

'That you needed a man to look after you. I dread to think what might have happened to us, if Sir Maurice had not discovered the truth about that man Prior. I daresay we should all have been murdered in our beds one night.'

'Peace, aunt! Remember that nothing is proved yet, and that tonight Mr Prior will still be sleeping under this roof with us.'

Beyond the formal garden lay the ruins of the abbey which had once occupied the site. Elisabeth loved the place in all its romantic, picturesque decay.

She had often gone there to be quiet when she was a little girl, and today she made her way there once again.

Her mind was in a turmoil. She could not believe that Robin had taken the miniatures, but there was a certain amount of circum-stantial evidence which pointed that way.

She was amazed at her reaction to what was, after all, a trivial affair. Why should she be so distressed because one of her servants was accused of stealing?

But this was happening to Robin, and she found she could not bear the thought of his being a rogue, and false to her.

She bowed her head into her lap, and shed a few tears, because she had allowed herself to become interested in a man who might prove to be a rogue.

She ought never to have left Town on this mad caper. She ought to have stayed where she was.

She tore at her handkerchief, and vowed that she would pack up and return to London on the morrow. Sir Maurice would no doubt follow, and she supposed that in due course, she would consent to be his wife.

She sniffed, feeling wretched, and two more tears squeezed out of her eyes to fall down her cheeks.

'My lady? Elisabeth, are you ill?'

Robin had entered the ruins unheard. He climbed up beside her, and gave her his handkerchief.

'They told me you were asking for me... I rode out to inspect a bridge that was reported dangerous. In heaven's name, what's wrong?'

FIVE

Elisabeth turned her shoulder on him, unwilling he should guess the cause of her tears. She said, 'A piece of dirt flew into my eye, and made it water. You should not have ridden out without telling me.'

'I thought the matter was urgent, and you were not up when I left.'

She lifted her shoulders, and let them drop. 'I wanted to use the small front parlour, but the key could not be found. I thought I asked you to find a locksmith to attend to it for me.'

'I'm sure you didn't ask me, or I'd have told you that I'd locked the door myself, and put the key above the lintel. Didn't I tell you?'

'Why should you have done such a thing?' Her mind said that he had done it to delay discovery of his theft of the miniatures, but her heart was beating so loudly that she could hardly hear his reply.

'The door kept flying open. The catch needs attention. There are a lot of Denys family papers in the secretaire, which ought to have been packed up and sent off to Mr Deeds weeks ago. I meant to deal with them straight away, but I have been rather busy.

I'm sorry. I'll clear out the papers and have the lock attended to immediately. There is no really good place to keep important papers in this house. Sir William used to keep money in an oak chest in the library, but the lock on that is defective, too.'

'You might have told me.'

He said, 'You weren't crying just because you couldn't get into the parlour?' He sounded amused.

'Of course not. We got into the room easily enough...' She could detect no change in his expression. Surely he must be innocent!

In a sudden change of mood, she put her hand on his arm, and smiled.

'I'm hungry, and I'm sure you haven't eaten properly today. Will you ask the maids to bring us something to eat, here in the ruins? We will have an alfresco meal, the two of us.'

'Madam, I...'

'A while ago you called me by my name.'

He avoided her eyes. 'Forgive me. For a moment I forgot my place.'

She jumped to her feet. 'Then I will give you an order, to use my name freely.'

'What, in public?'

'I'm not sure. Perhaps I'll give you permission to use it all the time, if you please me ... and you will please me by sending for some food and drink at once, for I am famished!'

He laughed, and obeyed her. Within a short space of time they were seated on convenient lumps of fallen masonry, eating chunks of veal and ham pie, and drinking home-brewed ale.

'Oh, this is good!' cried Elisabeth. 'Surely there is nothing better on a fine summer's day, than to eat good food in beautiful surroundings.' She sent him a mischievous glance. 'I forgot that you do not find this place beautiful!'

He smiled, too, looking around at the crumbling, windowless walls. Over all lay the hum of bees and the scent of wild wallflowers that clung to crevices in the masonry.

He said, 'No, I agree that it is beautiful.'

'Does the stolid Mr Prior actually admire something that is not producing food to feed the starving poor?'

To her delight, he laughed. 'One ruin is much like another,' he said. 'And although I must confess that I have never been tempted to write poetry in a ruin, as some of my contemporaries did ... yet I must admit they induce daydreams.'

She stared at him. 'You confess to having daydreams? Robin, I had not suspected it of you.'

He coloured up, and glanced away from her. 'You have a poor opinion of me, I fear.'

'No. I would not have said that. Did I hear you say your schoolfellows wrote poetry?

Where did you go to school?'

'You told me. In a barn.'

She bit her lip. 'Forgive me. Sometimes I let my tongue carry me away. Of course you went to a good school; it is written all over you. I suppose you went on to University?'

'I went to Oxford, like my grandfather before me. Don't look so surprised. People do have grandfathers, you know. The Priors are an ancient family, even if they are not noble.'

'I must apologise,' said Elisabeth. 'If I have wounded your feelings.'

'Not at all,' said Robin, at his coldest.

Elisabeth swallowed. 'I daresay you went on the Grand Tour of the Continent, as well?'

'Yes, but as I am sure you will have noticed, the Grand Tour failed to give me the polish of what you call a gentleman.'

'I am sorry,' she said, in a small voice. 'I think you are very much a gentleman.'

'Not,' he said, between his teeth, 'In Sir Maurice's eyes.'

'Well, Sir Maurice is ... different.'

'He is indeed.' His tone was still cool.

She stole a glance at him from under her lashes. He was sitting up very stiff and straight, looking as elegant as if he were in a London drawing-room. The freshly laundered white of his shirt and the lace at his cuffs contrasted with the smooth brown of his hands and sun-tanned face. It was not, of course, fashionable to have a tanned face, but at the moment Elisabeth found it extremely attractive.

She said, 'Tell me about your grandfather, and your farm.'

'My grandfather died three years ago, and then I took over the management of the farm from him. He half expected me to go soldiering – my father wanted me to be a soldier, apparently – but I prefer to build rather than to destroy. Besides, from the moment I was able to walk, I spent much of my time with him, going round the farms, listening while he talked business with our tenants...'

'You have tenants?' She failed to keep the surprise out of her voice.

'It is quite a large property, divided into three farms. I look after the Home Farm myself, and lease the two smaller farms to men who know what they are doing.'

'It is an estate, then?'

He gave her a straight look. 'There is no great house, or park ... nor any village on my land. We don't ape the nobility.'

She put her chin on her fist. 'But you make enough money from it to leave your farm when you like? You could move into the ranks of gentleman if you so wished.'

'I am satisfied with what I have, thank you. I have congenial neighbours, I frequently ride into Warwick on business, and sometimes I travel down to Oxford to stay with some of my old college friends, who have now turned into dons.'

'What of society in general?'

'I used to go up to London once or twice a year when grandfather was alive, for he wanted me to taste all the pleasures a young man should know, but I found Town life artificial, and monotonous. I will confess, though, to a liking for the theatre.'

'Perhaps you are human, after all.'

'My lady is pleased to make fun of me.'

'No.' She sighed. 'I am laughing at myself, I think. Did you never frequent Society gatherings when you went up to London?'

'Occasionally. I have two good friends who spend some time in Town every year…' Here he mentioned a couple of names known to her by repute. '…but I am always glad to return to the country.'

Elisabeth allowed her foot to peep out from under her skirts, as if by accident. His expression did not alter, but a muscle jumped in his throat.

Elisabeth's face took on a look of creamy satisfaction. He might pretend to be indifferent to her but he was not. There had been a hard, tight feeling about her heart, and now it eased away.

She said, 'I'm surprised that your grandfather did not arrange for you to marry young, to carry on the family line.'

He made a restless movement. 'He did

wish it, but … well, my mother was against me marrying young and I saw no one girl whom I liked above all the others, and so … like my father, perhaps I shall fall in love at first sight one day, and marry the girl no matter what anyone says.'

She absorbed that piece of information in silence. It had been delivered in a challenging tone, which she found affected her. Her heart was beating faster than usual, and she believed that her cheeks might be somewhat flushed. If she understood him correctly, then he was saying that he and she…

No, of course not.

Ridiculous!

On the other hand, it was not displeasing to sit beside him and speculate in idle fashion about love and marriage.

She said, 'Then you really didn't have any need to take the post of Steward here? You really ought to be back home, on your own property?'

'I had no need of the money,' he said. 'But it was a challenge, to see if I could bring order out of so much disorder. And, perhaps, I thought you needed me.'

She began to trace the pattern of the brocade in her skirt. 'Yes, I did need you, or someone like you. I fear you formed a very poor opinion of me to start with.'

'If I was rude … forgive me? At first you didn't seem to care at all about the villagers, or anything. But when I saw you walk into all those dreadful places ... and touch the children ... and talk to all the women ... believe me, I was filled with admiration for you.'

'You didn't show it.' She bent her head lower than ever.

'I did not think ... I was not sure...' He hesitated. Almost, he was stammering.

She looked up. Eyes of blue looked long into eyes of grey, and neither looked away.

A cuckoo started up its plaintive call nearby. Elisabeth started, and looked about her in a bemused way.

Then Robin got to his feet. He said there was much business awaiting him. He bowed, and left her.

She sat on for a long time, wondering if there were indeed so great a gap between a well-educated farmer, and a great heiress.

When she went back into the house, she was waylaid by the housekeeper.

It was about the missing miniatures. The housekeeper wished Elisabeth to know that it was impossible for any of her staff to have stolen them.

'I had not suspected them,' said Elisabeth, who had forgotten all about the miniatures.

The housekeeper looked relieved. 'I'm glad of that, my lady. I was going to show you the inventory, which proves that the miniatures were crossed off. They must have been taken out of the house before the servants – or any of us, for that matter – arrived at the Hall.'

'The inventory?'

'Yes, my lady. Mr Prior gave it to me the day I arrived, and naturally I checked the contents of every room as soon as I could. There were two miniatures on the inventory at first, over and above those we still have, but someone has crossed them off. Would you care to see the inventory for yourself?'

Elisabeth bit her lip. She supposed she ought to look at it, but she would very much rather not do so. It was all beginning to look as if Robin had taken the miniatures himself, and then crossed them out on the inventory before he handed it to the housekeeper. He had seemed to know his way around the house very well from the first … he had had plenty of time to remove the miniatures and his explanation for the locking of the door was plausible but not convincing.

She supposed that she could drop Robin a hint, so that he could replace the miniatures … but she had promised Sir Maurice that she would do nothing of the kind.

Oh, this was nonsense! Robin wouldn't stoop to steal! No never! She would stake her life on it.

She said to the housekeeper, 'Thank you

for telling me. I am glad that no blame can be attached to any of the servants. That will be all.'

'Heigh-ho!' sighed Mrs Marriott, yawning over her cup of chocolate at the breakfast-table. 'How much longer are we to linger in this wilderness, my love?'

'I like it here,' said Elisabeth.

'But the noise of the carpenters sawing … the hammering of the men on the roof…'

'These things are music to my ears,' said Elisabeth. 'I am sure this great old house appreciates the care and attention it is getting, after all those years of neglect.'

'But we could have gone to Bath while the workmen swarmed all over the place,' protested her aunt.

'I like it here,' said Elisabeth, once more. She sat with her chin on her fist, gazing out over the misty blue reaches of the Park.

Her aunt coughed. 'Are we a little distrait this morning? Are we, perhaps, allowing our thoughts to stray to a certain gentleman…?'

Elisabeth did not reply, for in truth she had been thinking of very little else but Robin … Robin … Robin…

Mrs Marriott smiled. 'Such a fine figure of a man.'

'Yes.'

'His air of command … he stands head and shoulders above the country bumpkins who have been visiting us … particularly the Hartleys. Squire Hartley is quite gross, isn't he? And his sons are country clods, as compared to our favourite, aren't they?'

'I think so, too,' said Elisabeth. 'But…'

'But, my love? Wherefore the hesitation?'

'I'm not sure.'

'Is it his lack of fortune that deters you?'

'N–no, I think not. Surely I have enough and to spare.'

'His family is old enough…'

'So he says.' And yet she sighed again.

Mrs Marriott smiled fondly at her niece. 'I daresay a woman needs a little time to consider before committing herself and her fortune to a man. But consider, niece, how little you think of your other suitors! At least this man is no mere clothes-hanger, no tattler of gossip. There is a certain force-fulness about him which I find admirable.'

'Yes,' said Elisabeth. She jumped to her feet, and went to the window, perhaps to cool her hot cheeks against the glass.

She thought that her aunt was right, and that Robin was the only real man of her acquaintance. The world might laugh if she married him. It would be said that he was a fortune-hunter, and that she had thrown herself away … but there would be compensations, surely, if she married a man whom she loved.

Mrs Marriott said, 'I daresay he will be

calling again soon. He is usually with us about noon, isn't he?'

'Who?'

'Why, Sir Maurice, of course. Who else have we been talking about all this time?'

'Why...' To cover her confusion Elisabeth tried and failed to open the window.

'Nothing works in this place,' observed her aunt, with mournful satisfaction. 'Better tell that man Prior to deal with it.'

'Yes,' said Elisabeth, in a strangled voice. 'Perhaps I will. We have arranged to discuss the estate in an hour's time.'

'But Sir Maurice will be here by then.'

'It will do Sir Maurice no harm to be denied my presence this once.'

'Perhaps you are right. Perhaps he is become a little too sure of himself.'

Elisabeth did not reply to that. To tell the truth, she had not thought very much about Sir Maurice this last week. In the first place, he had been much more restrained in his wooing of late, and she had begun to think she had been foolish to dread his presence. And in the second place, another man had occupied her thoughts to the exclusion of almost everything else.

She wondered what Robin was doing at that very moment. Perhaps he was down in the village, overseeing men on repairs there. Perhaps he had returned, and might even now be working in the library.

She thought she might wander along to the library now, to see if there were any book on the shelves which might please her.

Her footman entered with a note on a silver salver, before she could put her resolve into action.

The note was from Sir Maurice, who apologised for not being able to call upon her that day. He had recently moved from the village inn into the house of an acquaintance of his who shared his taste for gambling. To the best of his host's knowledge, there was no family called Prior farming in any substantial way in Warwickshire. Sir Maurice thought it best, therefore, to ride into Warwick that day, to pursue his enquiries about the man calling himself Robin Prior.

Mrs Marriott looked over her niece's shoulder, and read the note, too.

'There!' said Mrs Marriott. 'I always said there was something very odd about that man Prior.' She nodded dismissal to the footman.

Elisabeth put a hand to her mouth, because it was trembling, and she did not wish her aunt to observe it.

'What are you going to do, Elisabeth? The man is an imposter.'

'I must speak to him about it, I suppose.'

'If you take my advice, you will leave it till Sir Maurice arrives. Where would we be, without that dear man, I wonder?'

'In blissful ignorance, I suppose.'

Mrs Marriott was shocked. 'You don't mean that, my dear!'

'No, perhaps not.' Elisabeth felt tears threaten, and clenched her hands into fists. 'Well, shall we pack up and move on to Bath tomorrow?'

'I will tell the housekeeper...'

'No, wait. I can't leave with everything unsettled about the tenants on the estate, and the bridge, and the repairs.'

'Sir Maurice will find someone to undertake all those little problems for you.'

'Perhaps. Yes, perhaps that would be best. But...' She put her hand to her head. 'I think perhaps I'm developing a headache. I'll go and lie down for a while, aunt, and then I can think what I ought to do for the best. Perhaps I ought to write to Mr Deeds, and ask him to find me a good steward for this place. I believe I accepted responsibility for my tenants when I signed the lease of this place, and if I dismiss Robin ... Mr Prior...'

'If, indeed, that is his name.'

Elisabeth went out into the hall on dragging feet. She pulled the door of the parlour to behind her, and tested it. It was quite true that occasionally the catch did not slip into place easily. Robin had spoken the truth about that. The footman was in the hall, chatting in a low voice to one of the maids.

Elisabeth had the uncomfortable feeling that the footman knew everything that went on in the house. Again she thought about dismissing him, and again she did nothing about it.

She walked across the hall to the library doors, the footman held them open for her, and she went in. This room, unlike the parlour, was in the stone-built wing, and the windows were tall and wide. One of them was open, and the place smelled fresh and clean.

The leather of the heavy armchair by the fireplace shone, and the spines of the books, in their tooled leather bindings, provided a pleasant, muted background to Robin's tall figure.

He had been out riding, and must have come in only that moment, for he was still wearing riding boots, and had thrown his crop and hat onto the table in front of him.

He rose as she entered, and pulled out a chair for her, with a smile.

She blinked. He had sent for some of his clothes, and instead of his old buff coat and buckskin breeches, he was dressed today in blue velvet. There were silver buttons on the coat, and French lace at his wrists. His waistcoat was embroidered with silver flowers, and his breeches were of the same velvet as his coat.

She felt something lodge in her throat.

One part of her wanted to throw herself into his arms and beg him to elope with her, and the other half wanted to pick up his riding crop and slash him across the face with it.

'Elisabeth … I had not hoped to see you so early this morning.'

She sank into the chair and leaned back, looking up at him. 'Did I give you permission to use my name?'

The smile left his face. 'I thought you had.'

She looked away from him. 'That was yesterday. I am a very changeable person, you know.'

He returned to his side of the desk, and sat down.

She said, 'I ought perhaps to have asked my aunt to be present at this interview, but I wished to spare you that. Whatever your motives, you have served me well enough since you came … I suppose.'

He was wary. 'I am not sure I understand you.'

'Is it necessary that you should?' Elisabeth knew how to be haughty when it suited her, and now she used that knowledge to cover the fact that she had been hurt.

'I suppose not.' He looked puzzled. 'You employed me for a purpose...'

'And perhaps because it amused me to trifle with you a while. After all, the country is thin of company...' Here she gave a delicate yawn, and hid it behind her fan. She was rewarded by seeing him flush, and look down. She was glad that she could hurt him so easily ... and then she was angry because by hurting him, she found she was hurting herself.

'Enough of that,' she said. 'I am told that you have lied to me, that you took this situation under false pretences.'

He stood up, walked away from her to look out of the window. He said, 'It is true that I had no need for the money ... but then, you knew that, already. I am not sure what you mean, precisely.'

She simply could not force the words out, and say that he had lied about his name.

He turned his head, waiting for her to speak. The breeze blew in through the window, and stirred papers on the desk.

Elisabeth lifted her eyes to the portrait of Sir William over the fireplace. Silently, she begged him for advice and help.

As if in answer to her prayer, Robin spoke. 'It is true that I have not been entirely open with you about myself in some respects, but I thought then – and I still think – that I took the right course. If anyone suffers for it, then it is I alone. I assure you, my lady, that I have served you faithfully and to the best of my ability, and will continue to do so, so long as you have need of me.'

'Will you swear as much on the Bible?'

He looked about him at the crowded

bookshelves. 'Of course. There is bound to be one here somewhere, I suppose.'

She felt herself relax. She looked up at Sir William's painted face, and sent him a vote of thanks. Surely now she could trust Robin, no matter what Sir Maurice said. To her mind Robin's voice carried conviction.

'I believe you,' she said. 'Although I do not like secrets, yet I will trust you a while longer.'

He grimaced. 'You cannot like secrets less than I do.'

'Then why...?'

'I promise I will tell you one day, when I am no longer your Steward. Does that satisfy you?'

She gave him her hand. 'I ought not to do so, Robin ... but I will sit on my curiosity a little longer.'

He held her hand in both of his, as he had done once before. She willed him to pull her close to him, to kiss her.

'Elisabeth!' He bent his head to kiss her fingers, but this time he exerted no pressure, and her hand slipped away from his as soon as the caress was done.

Yet she did not move away. She smiled at him, and her voice was soft as she rebuked him. 'Did I give you leave to call me by my name?'

'No,' he said, with a mixture of boldness and shyness, unusual to him. 'I took the liberty, but if you wish it, I will apologise.'

'I do not wish it now, although I cannot answer for how I will feel later on today … or tomorrow.'

He bowed and said, 'I understand. Now, do you wish to discuss business for half an hour, or have you had enough of my company for today?'

SIX

It was a fine, moonlit night, and Elisabeth could settle to nothing. She rang for her cloak, and went out of the house to saunter among the ruins. When she turned to look at the house, the ground floor windows streamed with light from the parlour in which her aunt was sitting ... and from the library where Robin was working on his plans.

Perhaps she hoped that Robin would see her walking among the ruins, and would come out to join her, in his splendid velvet clothes.

She was in a strange mood; one moment she wanted to clap her hands for joy and run wild, and the next she felt sad and listless.

She looked up at the great white globe of the moon, hanging low above the trees, and thought how pleasant it would be to stroll around with a man's arm about your waist, and your head on his shoulder.

Perhaps Robin would go further than speaking her Christian name soon. Perhaps he would tell her that she had ears like shells, or a swan-like neck ... she had been told those things a dozen times by other men, but if Robin were to say so, surely it would mean something to her for the first time!

There! Was that a footfall? Was it the ghost which was supposed to haunt the ruins or had the door onto the terrace opened and shut?

She felt sure it was Robin, come to join her.

She was poised to run from him, suddenly shy.

But if she ran away, he might think she did not really wish him to join her.

No. She would stay where she was, and wait for him to join her.

Her eyes and ears were alert. She thought she saw a tall shadow cross the moonlit sward in her direction, but she could not be sure.

Someone laughed, softly, close by.

She started, hand to breast, for she had not expected Robin to laugh like that. It was the laugh of a man scenting victory, and she had not yet given Robin sufficient encouragement for that.

She drew back into the shadows, and held her breath. He must soon pass through the empty, gaping doorway … and then she would see him, clear in the moonlight.

Another low laugh and she felt a frisson of fear, for it did not seem to her that Robin laughed like that, ever. She risked a glance back at the house, and thought she saw a tall figure pass across the windows of the library between her and the candles. So, Robin was still within and he had not come to join her in the ruins.

Her heart was beginning to hammer unsteadily.

If the man in the ruins was not Robin, then who was it?

'I have you now!' A tall man enveloped her in his arms from behind. She cried out in fear, and tried to fight him off.

'Would you show your claws then?' He laughed again, and this time she knew that laugh.

'Unhand me, sir!'

'Not so fast! First, a token from your lips!'

He was a tall man and strong, and although Elisabeth was no weakling she had been taken by surprise. She found herself lifted from the ground, and whirled about. One moment she was staring up into the face which was transformed by the shadows into that of a grinning devil ... and the next his lips came down on hers, and she felt as if the very life was being crushed out of her.

She could not bear it! She beat at his head, knocking off his tricorne hat, and unsettling his wig. He lifted his lips from hers at last, and when he did, she arched her body in his grasp till he, unbalanced, was forced to let her wriggle out of his arms.

'Elisabeth!'

'How dare you!' With all the weight of her body behind her, Elisabeth delivered a ringing blow to his ear.

Her mouth felt as if it were swollen, and she felt sick with fear and shame that he should take advantage of her so easily.

'Damn your eyes!' swore Sir Maurice. 'I'll tame you yet!' He reached for her, and she took a pace back, breathing hard. Her cloak slipped off her shoulders, the fastening torn away. He said, 'I thought you wanted to be wooed in the ruins ... so romantic, you said. But if you want to fight, then I'm your man for that, too!'

She was breathing hard, feeling behind her for the wall. 'If you come one step closer, I'll...'

'What will you do, my dear? Eh, but you've the look of a witch about you in this light, with your hair tumbling about your shoulders ... come here!'

'Never!'

Like a hare she darted for the nearest dark shadow, and then was through an archway, turning in her tracks, doubling back. He kept up with her well. She began to feel hunted. She thought she had lost him, and stole silently forward ... and then he shot out at her, with his hand outstretched...

Terrified, she twisted away and ran, expecting at any minute to feel him grab her from behind ... but instead she heard him swear as he stumbled over a stone half-buried in the sward. She was half-way to the house, with her skirts hampering her, and her breath tearing at her throat ... he was gaining on her again ... he was swifter than she ... but she was nearly there...

She reached the door into the Hall, and wrenched it open. Once within, she swung the door to, but he had his foot there, and began to use his superior weight to force the door open.

'Help me!' she cried, her voice hoarse. 'Thomas!' Where was that footman?

Instead, it was Robin who opened the door of the library and came out, looking alarmed. He was holding a branched candlestick high in his hand. It was late. Presumably most of the servants had retired for the night, but the footman ought to have been still on duty in the hall ... and was not.

Seeing Robin, she relaxed her grip on the door, and Sir Maurice was able to force his way in. He ignored Robin, to bend over her.

'So, you like to play games, do you? We will play again tomorrow night, shall we?'

'No! I tell you ... go!'

Robin was looking wooden and furious, at one and the same time. He was also looking badly shaken. Undoubtedly he had mis-interpreted what he had seen, and thought she had been leading Sir Maurice on in love play.

She looked down, and found that the front of her silk bodice had been ripped open, and that her hair was indeed about her shoulders. She had also torn her skirt. She wanted to cry, and also to swear.

Robin bowed, and said that if she required anything else, he would be in the library. There was fire in his eyes, but ice in his voice.

'Stay!' she said, as he made to withdraw. 'I want you to summon the servants, so as to see Sir Maurice off the premises. I did not know he would be calling this evening...'

'No more you did,' said Sir Maurice, with one of his wide smiles. 'But I caught sight of you as you walked in the ruins, and I remembered how romantic you thought them ... and I thought you would be pleased if I joined you...'

'Pleased!' She tried to hold the torn silk of her bodice together.

'And then,' said Sir Maurice, widening his smile even more, 'The moonlight bewitched us, did it not? I will call again in the morning, Elisabeth, to make sure that you are fully recovered.'

'I shall not be at home.'

'Oh, I think you will,' said Sir Maurice, with a lift of his eyebrow in Robin's direction. 'I think I shall have some interesting news for you. Till tomorrow.' He bowed and left.

Robin locked and barred the front door without comment. He did not look at Elisabeth, and she understood from his silence and from the rigid set of his shoulders that he had accepted Sir Maurice's version of the affair. Had she dreamed that she had seen his eyes flash with the fire of jealousy?

She said, 'Robin, I did not ask him to meet me in the ruins … and I did not wish him to make love to me…'

'No, my lady?' He gave her a look of cold disdain.

Too proud to plead with him, Elisabeth fled upstairs to her room.

'Well, my dear?' Sir Maurice bowed over her hand as if he were making an ordinary morning call.

She turned her shoulder on him to show that she was still angry.

'I wouldn't have received you this morning, if it weren't…'

'…that you wished to know how I'd fared in Warwick? Well, if you imagine the worst, then I dare say you'll not be far off.'

'What is the worst?'

'Your steward's name is not Prior. A family of that name did once farm land about twenty miles south of Warwick, but the last of the line died some years ago, and the family is now extinct. Your man is an imposter. Knowing there is now no male heir to challenge his use of the name, your steward has taken it for himself.'

Elisabeth's head drooped. 'Yet I believe he meant no harm.'

Sir Maurice shrugged. 'It depends what you mean by harm.'

'He admitted there was a secret in his past.'

'I daresay there is. Perhaps he is some bastard of the Priors, who has taken the name illegally.'

Elisabeth's face flamed, and she looked away from Sir Maurice. 'Yet he had served me well.'

'By stealing your miniatures?'

'We do not know that he has, and I for one do not believe it. It would be out of character.'

'I'll admit he gives the impression of being an honest man, but then I believe most successful villains manage to put on an appearance of honesty. It is part of their stock in trade, so to speak. You must dismiss the man, Elisabeth.'

'No, I'll not do that. I need him here, and if I keep an eye on him, he can do no harm.'

'He could rob you blind, and you none the wiser. What knowledge do you have of business affairs? Couldn't he hoodwink you a dozen times a day?'

She swallowed. 'Very well. I'll get Mr Deeds to find me a man to replace Robin...'

'You call him by his Christian name?'

She was dismissive. 'What else, if his last name is not Prior? Sir Maurice, I am grateful to you for discovering the truth, but...'

'You don't sound grateful. You sound angry.'

'Perhaps I am. It's not pleasant to be taken in by someone.'

'No more it is. Then you'll let me dismiss him today?'

She wandered about the room, touching this and that. She bit her lip. She played with her fan.

Sir Maurice lounged in his chair, watching her.

She said at last, 'I'll speak with him today, yes.'

'In my presence? I'd prefer that, Elisabeth. He might so easily deceive you again.'

'You may stay here if you will, while I go to speak with him. I'll not need you in the room with me. He's not the sort of person to take advantage of me by moonlight, as you did.'

Sir Maurice laughed. 'Touche! But tell me, did not your heart beat faster, and your pulse race when I kissed you?'

'No. I detest force.'

'You need a touch of the whip now and then, Elisabeth, and you know it!'

'No. That is not the way to win me.'

He smiled, and smoothed his chin. It

seemed he did not believe her.

'Sir Maurice, I bid you goodday!'

'Not till you've had your interview with the imposter, my dear.'

'Oh, very well. Wait here for me.'

She went across the hall, and into the library. As usual, Robin was working on some papers at the desk. She confronted him before he could fairly rise to his feet to greet her.

She said, 'I believe I have discovered your secret, sir. Your name is no more Prior than mine is.'

He put down his quill with care. 'Who told you that?'

'Does it matter? Sir Maurice has been making enquiries about you.'

'Ah, I see.' He had gone pale, but not lost his composure.

'You don't deny it?'

'It is half true. My mother's name was Prior.'

She glared at him. 'So you are a bastard, then. You use your mother's name because you have no legal right to any other.'

His lips thinned. 'No. My father and mother were legally married, and normally I use his name as a matter of course, but…'

There was a pause. He took his eyes off her, and frowned into space.

'Well?' she prompted him. 'What is your father's name?'

'I have a very good reason for not telling you, at the moment. Lady Elisabeth, I didn't seek to deceive you from any ulterior motive. I have placed myself in an impossible position. I have been lying awake at nights, wondering how the devil … but that's nothing to the case. If it weren't for the job that's crying out to be done here, I'd throw up my position here, and leave. And then…'

'I think you must do that, anyway.'

There was a short, strained silence. 'Yes,' he said at last. 'You are right. I'll find a replacement for myself as soon as may be. I must admit I'll be glad to be done with this masquerade, in many ways.'

'And I, too. It can't be over quickly enough to please me.'

She swept out without another look at him. She wanted to go straight up to her room to cry, but Sir Maurice waylaid her in the hall.

'Well, did he admit it?'

'Partly. I've told him to leave, and he has agreed to find a replacement for himself as soon as possible.'

'Elisabeth, you ought to have shown him the door at once.'

'Why? I'd then be entirely without protection from you.'

'Such protection as he can offer, is worse than nothing.'

'Have done! I won't turn him out like a

beggar, just because he lied about bearing an honourable name.'

'What if I can prove that he is a thief?'

She started. She had forgotten about the miniatures. She said, 'I do not think you can do that.'

'But if I do?'

'Why ... that will be another matter.'

He had grasped her hand. She wrenched it away from him and ran up the stairs to her room.

She tried to put Robin out of her mind, and failed. His image crept unbidden into her mind whenever she was not actively involved in doing something else.

Then she would perhaps stray to a window and looking out, would see Robin directing men at work to clear the overgrown knot garden ... or watch with bated breath while he climbed a ladder to investigate affairs on the roof.

He was everywhere, it seemed; and if he himself were not present, then he left evidence that he had been in every place before her. The chimneys ceased to smoke, and the floorboards began to gleam with polish, as did the furniture. The heavy gilt frames of the Denys family pictures in the Gallery were burnished, and instead of the smell of decay, the pleasant odour of beeswax scented the air.

The housekeeper had long lived there-abouts. When she was very young she had been employed as a housemaid at the Hall. In the years between she had married, pro-duced a family, lost her husband, and was now living in an overcrowded cottage with one of her sons and his young family. The woman was only too delighted to remove to more spacious quarters at the Hall, and to impart her housewifely knowledge to the newly-employed staff.

Somewhat to her surprise, Elisabeth found that learning how to run the Hall gave her pleasure. There was satisfaction to be found in re-arranging furniture, and planning new colour schemes. She had not Robin's love of order for its own sake, but nevertheless she had to admit that the life of a country gentlewoman had its compen-sations.

One moment she decided to spend the rest of the summer at the Hall, and the next she'd remember that Robin must soon be leaving, and that in any case he was a false knave … and then she would tell her aunt that in a day or two they would perhaps move on to Bath, or back to London.

The worst hours were at night, when she was alone in her great bed. She would drift in and out of sleep, dozing and dreaming…

Even in sleep she was haunted by images of Robin. Sometimes she would wake with a cry, and put her hands to her head, vainly trying to remember something of import-ance that she had discovered in her dreams. But all that remained was the conviction that she had dreamed of Robin ... or not of Robin, perhaps, but of someone like him ... much younger ... different in some way. And that it was important that she remember what it was she had dreamed.

Some nights she was afraid to go to bed, but would sit up late, playing cards with her aunt, or reading doggedly through some dry tome from the library.

Mrs Marriott remarked on her niece's heavy eyes, saying that no-one slept well in the country.

'It's not that,' said Elisabeth, listlessly. She threw aside the letters she had received that morning from Town. There was a note from her old steward, in a wavering hand, saying that he hoped to be on his legs again shortly ... invitations ... gossip.

She picked up a newspaper, only to throw that aside, too, a moment later. She studied one of Robin's estimates for repairs. It went into a lot of detail. She had a feeling that the repairs would be carried out within the estimate both for time and money. She dreaded to think how matters would go on without him. It was ridiculous to think of his being a cheat and a thief!

She wished she were able to settle to

something for more than a few minutes at a time.

She said to her aunt, 'Perhaps I will send to the stables and tell them to saddle my mare. I'd like to see how they are getting on with the repairs to the bridge. Robin said it ought to be rebuilt in stone, because it would be an economy in the long run.'

'I hope he is not overburdening your brain with business. I'm surprised that Mr Prior should trouble you with such nonsense, and I'm sure Sir Maurice would never do so.'

'Now that is another thing. Aunt, Sir Maurice has called twice, and you have failed to chaperone me.'

'I did not think, my dear, that you wished to be chaperoned when Sir Maurice called.'

Elisabeth grimaced. 'Well, I do. The man is...'

'Masterful?' Mrs Marriott twinkled at Elisabeth. 'Do you object to that?'

'Yes. No. Oh, I do not know what I think, except that I have no mind to be compromised by him.'

'You ought to marry soon.'

'Perhaps I shall live and die an old maid.'

'I don't think you'd like that, my love.'

Elisabeth laughed. 'No, perhaps not.' She went to the window, and began to drum on it with her fingers. 'The sky is clearing. I think I will go walk in the gardens a while.'

Elisabeth sent for her cloak, and went out

into the pale sunshine. She walked through the knot garden, observing how the gardeners were trimming the ancient borders. Then she went through a door in a wall, into the warmth of what had once been a herb garden, and was surrounded by high walls, and lined with fruit trees.

She sank onto a bench in a sheltered corner, and found herself dozing. She was short of sleep, and the sun relaxed her. She arranged herself in a more comfortable position, and allowed herself to drift off again. As she slid into sleep she wished that this time at least she would not dream of Robin...

In her dream she was happy. She was high up on the back of a horse, being led round the paddock by a fair-haired youth in shirt-sleeves. She was a little frightened of the horse but although the boy knew that, he was telling her that she must relax and trust him, for nothing was going to go wrong.

She woke with a start, and this time as she snatched at the memory, some of it stayed with her ... and the shred of memory grew into certainty as she found herself looking up into Robin Prior's face.

'You,' she said, stretching out her hand to him. 'You were here at the Hall one summer, years ago ... you taught me to ride again!'

SEVEN

The hard line of his mouth relaxed. 'That's right. You'd had a bad fall off a horse the year before, hadn't you?'

'...and my father had forbidden me to ride again till my back stopped aching, and then I found I was too frightened...'

'But so courageous! You set your little chin, and commanded me to lift you onto the highest horse, and no-one else guessed that you were shaking inside...'

'You knew, though. You were so kind to me, walking the horse round and round the paddock, with me clinging on by my knees...'

He laughed. 'You were such a tiny mite, but you insisted that you must ride my horse because it was the best...'

'Why didn't you remind me that we'd met before?'

'If you'd forgotten, how could I remind you, especially after I became your steward?'

She frowned, remembering the troubles that now lay between them. She sighed, and so did he. He was holding a folded note in his hand.

She said, 'Won't you sit down awhile? I am

115

sad today. Let us talk of the old days, when we were happy.'

He held out the note. 'Sir Maurice sent me to you with this note.'

'He has no right to order you about.'

'I thought he had. He made it clear that he had your authority ... that you and he would shortly be joined in matrimony.'

'Perhaps. I don't know. Perhaps I will remove to Bath next week. Heigh-ho, but the world is a chancy place! Let us forget it for a while. You have not answered my question as to how you came to be here when I was nine ... ten?'

'You were just ten years old. There were quite a few people staying here at the Hall that summer. You and your father, and some aunts... Sir William had invited some of his relations and old friends. I lost count. It was all rather bewildering for a lad of my age.'

'But you were grown up!'

He laughed. 'I may have seemed old to you then, but I was only fifteen at the time. Sir William had some whim ... it came to nothing, of course ... but I was taken out of school and brought here for a month ... and then dismissed when he had tired of my face.'

'What did he want with you?'

'Oh...' Robin was vague. 'He thought of adopting some promising lad ... paying for his education, perhaps. There were several

116

of us boys here at the time ... but of course nothing came of it.'

'I am sorry.'

'Don't be. My mother and grandfather were not paupers, you know.'

Here they were, back on dangerous ground. She bit her lip, and cast about her for some way of changing the subject. The folded note in Robin's hand caught her eye, and she held out her hand for it.

He handed it over, she broke the seal, and read it.

'Elisabeth, my dear,' she read.

'I am in a fair way to getting the proof you wanted. Keep the imposter with you in the garden, till I come. Maurice.'

For one wild moment she thought of warning Robin, of telling him to flee ... and then common sense took over. If Robin had indeed stolen the miniatures ... and it was plainly ridiculous to think that he might have done so ... then it would not be right to let him get away with the crime.

She said, with an assumption of carelessness, 'It is nothing. He wishes to be sure of speaking with me this morning, but I don't know whether I will or no. I am a little tired of him.'

She crumpled up the note, and let it fall to the ground. Robin grimaced, picked up the note, and placed it in his pocket. He did not do this because he wished to read the note, but because he disliked untidiness.

At once she was on fire lest he read the note, and suspect that the Law was after him.

She said, 'I've been dreaming much of you, of late. It seems to me that we must have been together a great deal that summer long ago, for when I wake I retain snatches of memory ... which tease me because I can't make sense of them.'

She resolved to be charming, to captivate him. She would hold him at her side, as she knew well how to hold a man.

Robin put his arm along the bench at the back of her, and smiled.

He said, 'What can I tell you? You were much younger than I, and closely guarded. There was your father, and your nurse, and I think there was a governess, always about you. You only had to express a wish, for everyone in the household to tumble over themselves to do your bidding, from Sir William down to the humblest groom.'

'I was very spoilt, doubtless.' She looked at him from under her lashes.

He would not flirt with her, even now. 'Yes, a little, I suppose. But you were kind, too, and loving. I remember you threw your arms round my neck and comforted me when my hunter had to be destroyed.'

'I can't remember that! Oh, I wish I could!'

'There was a race,' he prompted her. 'Do you remember that? There were some eight or nine of us, adults as well as youngsters. Sir William laid out a course around the outside of the Park, and there were wagers taken and laid...'

'But not by you! Surely you did not bet?'

'No, but you did.' He grinned at her. 'Don't you remember that you bet your fur muff that I'd win?'

'I remember that muff. Yes, and I think I remember the race, although it is very hazy. Didn't I give someone the prize ... was it you? Could it have been you?'

'Yes, I won. My hunter was a fine lass, and I missed her bitterly.'

'There was an accident?'

'One of my friends took her out one morning without permission. He put her at a gate so clumsily that she caught her leg. Ah well, it's best not to dwell on such things now.'

'What did you do to the boy who lamed your horse?'

'Beat him to pulp behind the stables, of course. We both felt better for the fight, and we remain friends to this day. You remember I told you I'd gone on the Grand Tour? Well, I went with that lad and his tutor. He is married now, and is standing for Parliament at the next election. He is a very serious fellow nowadays.'

She smiled. 'So are you, I think.'

'I am aware that you prefer more amusing companionship…'

'Did I say so? Do you think I care only for fops and rakes?'

'I don't know. One moment I think you have a heart, and the next…'

'Am I so changeable?' She had intended to keep up her light-hearted manner, but somehow her voice betrayed her into a sob.

'Yes. You are like an April day, all smiles and tears. How can a man tell where he is with you?'

'Or with you, for that matter. One moment you are as stiff as a poker and call me "my lady", and the next…'

'You forget I'm your steward.'

'For the moment, only.'

'I have written to Mr Deeds, asking him to find some clerk who could perhaps take charge of your household until such time as a trained man can be found to take on the post of steward.'

'And then?' Her breathing had quickened.

'And then I will remove to the inn, or to Warwick.'

'And then?' She put her hand to her heart.

'I will take the liberty of calling on you one morning, to explain everything that may have puzzled you in the past.'

He picked up her hand, and put it to his lips. She tightened her clasp on his fingers.

She said, 'Robin, tell me now!'

His eyelids contracted. 'Don't tempt me, Elisabeth. I know what I am doing, and believe me, it is best that I leave your employ and your roof before anything further is said between us.'

'I have a good reason for asking.'

'And I an equally good reason for declining to answer.'

She snatched her hand away. 'You don't wish to please me. You don't care for me. You think I'm not to be trusted, that I'm a heartless flirt...'

And here she stopped, both hands pressed to her heart, for she had remembered that she was in some sort playing a part, holding Robin here in the garden till such time as Sir Maurice was ready to move against him. She despised herself. She half rose from her seat, and then sank back again, because if she ended this interview now, she might never see Robin again, and the thought of parting with him was terrible to her.

'Elisabeth ... don't play with me!'

'I'm not playing,' said Elisabeth, and realised that this was the truth. 'I merely want to know how you feel about me. I know it's unseemly for a woman to ask a man to his face...'

'You know how I feel!' His voice was low and fierce. He did not look at her.

'No, I do not. For all I know, you took the

position of steward here because you thought... I don't know what you may have thought, but when you saw how unprotected I was...'

'Yes, it was that, partly. I recognised your crest on the panels of your coach, when you passed me on the hill above the ford. I knew that Lady Elisabeth Silverwood was due to arrive at Denys Hall that day, and when I saw the way Sir Maurice engineered the accident at the ford, I rode back to see if you needed any assistance ... though I told myself that it was most unlikely that you would remember me.'

'You ought to have reminded me.'

'I thought that there were many men who would have tried to force their acquaintance on you in such fashion ... knowing that you were rich and without protection. I decided that it would not be right to take advantage of you in your unprotected state, but that perhaps I could recall myself to you later, when you were in a position to deny the acquaintance if you so wished.'

'I wish you had told me. I would never have offered you the post of steward, if I had known!'

He laughed, unhappily. 'That occurred to me, too. I am not ordinarily so impulsive, but the words were out before I knew what I'd offered to do ... and then I thought that perhaps it was only right and proper that I should try to do something about the estate...'

'Why? What was it to you?'

He checked, and then said, rather too smoothly, 'Nothing. I meant, merely, that I had so much, and these poor people here had so little.'

For the first time, she felt he had lied. She was also feeling hurt that he had not said he had taken the post for her sake. Yes, that really did hurt.

He said, 'But then I realised that by taking the post, I could be near you day and night ... maybe only for a little while...' He stopped, in some confusion. 'Forgive me, I ought not to have said that.'

'Why not? Perhaps that is what I wanted to hear.'

'How can that be? You are the Lady Elisabeth Silverwood, a great heiress, and I ... nothing.' Tears came into her eyes.

'Elisabeth,' he said, low down. 'Don't cry. I can't bear to see you cry. How can I make love to you now?'

'Do you wish to do so?'

'You know it.'

'I want to hear you say it, clearly.'

He raised his hands and let them fall. 'A few more days...'

Elisabeth twisted her hands together. He did not know that there was no more time left. Ah, if only she could think of some way of making him declare himself, then perhaps she would be able to protect him from Sir Maurice!

The beginning of an idea started into her mind, and she clapped her hands over her eyes, trying to think.

'Elisabeth, my love…'

He had dared to put his arm about her shoulders. He thought she was in distress, and indeed she was, though not in the way he imagined.

She decided that she must put her idea into practice. If she did not act now, she might never have another opportunity of discovering whether or not a man could love her for herself alone. As for the deceit – and it did mean that she would have to deceive him – it was nothing compared to the fact, which he had admitted several times, that he was deceiving her about his name and station.

She said in a trembling voice, 'I must tell you… I can't let you go on believing that I'm a great heiress. The truth is that the fortune my father left me was not always in Mr Deeds' capable hands … there was speculation … leading to heavy losses.'

He stared at her blankly. 'But everyone knows…'

She hid her face from him again, partly because she was ashamed to act such a part, and partly for fear that he would not react the way she wanted him to.

She said, 'You know how it is … if a girl is not ugly, and it is known that she has inherited some money, then rumour multiplies the amount. And indeed my father did leave me a reasonable fortune, but as I said, it has dwindled with bad handling over the years.'

He took a deep breath. 'Well, you still have much property…'

'I have put the palazzo in Rome on the market, though I doubt if it will fetch much. The apartment in Paris will have to be let or sold, too. As for the house in London, I fear I have been running into debt there, by keeping it open and fully staffed all the year round. Of course I have tried to cut back, to retrench everywhere … but it is not easy, especially since my aunt seems to have no idea of how to act in straitened circumstances.'

'Indeed, she talks of your spending large sums every night at the gaming tables.'

'I have been trying to recoup my fortunes, which was very silly of me.'

He looked stunned. 'Then when you inherited Sir William's money…'

'It was a windfall. I cleared some of my debts and left Town, hoping to be able to live quietly here.'

'And I made you pour money and yet more money into the estate … for repairs …

rebuilding … telling your tenant farmers they need not pay any rent this year… God in heaven, Elisabeth! Why did you allow me to throw your money away like that?'

'You told me that if I put money into the estate, it would pay its way within a couple of years, and I wanted to please you.'

'What folly!'

In his agitation he began to stride up and down, his hand to his head. Suddenly he stopped, and struck one hand against the other. His chin looked very square.

'Elisabeth, when I thought you were so far above me, it seemed impossible that I could speak but now I can, and I will.'

'Pray do,' said Elisabeth, trying to look meek.

'My land is not encumbered by debts, and I have nearly a thousand pounds in the Funds. You must allow me to advance you what you require to live in civilised fashion until such time as this estate can begin to pay its own way.'

'On what security?' asked Elisabeth, even more meek.

'On none. On your person. On whatever you will. Elisabeth, in God's name, do you think I could stand by and see you lack for anything? Give me your note of hand … or a kiss, if you would not think that too much…?'

'What sort of kiss?'

He took his seat at her side, and turned her to face him. 'I will take as much as you are prepared to give. Be warned, Elisabeth. Do not offer more than you want to give me … freely … without compulsion.'

'You would never compel me to anything, would you?'

'I'd try not to do so, although there are times when you drive me mad, and I have hard work not to…' He swallowed, and did not complete the sentence.

'Tell me,' said Elisabeth, and placed one hand on the soft blue of his coat.

'I have hard work not to carry you off back home,' he said, with a rush. 'To pick you up just as you are, and gallop back home with you in front of me, your arms about my neck … as they were when I rescued you from the ford. We'd come back to the Home Farm in the early evening, perhaps, and my housekeeper and the maids would all come out to make you welcome, and there would be home-brewed ale in a tankard for me, and a glass of wine for you … for you must know that my father laid down a notable cellar of wines.'

'You live well?'

'My grandfather and my mother always insisted on the best of everything, and I do not think you would feel it a disgrace to sit at my table.'

'I am sure I would not,' said Elisabeth, and

her hand strayed up to his collar, while his arm went round her waist.

'The dining-room is oak-panelled with a great stone fireplace. The main rooms were remodelled by my father, to please my mother, with some fine plasterwork on the ceilings and mahogany furniture which he chose for her in London. He laid out the flower garden for her, too. It is enclosed in high walls, like this one. There are doves in the dovecote, and dogs ... and I'd gentle a horse for you to ride.'

'I'd like that,' said Elisabeth, with perfect truth.

He reddened. 'We'd have to be married first, of course. I couldn't take you straight back home.' He checked himself. 'I'm day-dreaming again, aren't I? None of this could ever come to pass.'

'Could it not?'

Elisabeth lifted her face, and smiled at him. She felt sleepy, and happy and excited, all at once. She knew that there was still something missing, though.

'Are you sure, Elisabeth?'

'Yes, I am very sure.'

She slid her hand between the heavy black ribbon that bound back his hair, and the cravat about his neck. Still he hesitated, though she could feel his arm shift, so that she lay more closely against him.

'Oh, Elisabeth...!'

He touched her forehead with his lips, lightly, beneath the dark curls. She shivered with delight, and her fingers tightened at the back of his neck, wanting a closer contact with him. Oh, the warm, smooth skin of his throat, and the strength of his arms about her! She had never felt like this before, she was sure of that ... and yet he was not crushing her, or hurting her in any way.

He kissed her temples ... her eyes, and her ears. She turned her head up to his, and tried to kiss him, at the same time as he was kissing her.

At last their lips met and brushed against each other. They both drew back, a little afraid of what was happening to them.

He put one hand up to smooth back the curl on her forehead, and then, slowly ... tenderly ... bent his head to kiss her lips again.

This time it was no half-accidental caress. Their lips met, clung, and moved together. His arms tightened about her, and she moved towards him at the same moment, her arm going about his neck, drawing him down to her.

She did not open her eyes even when he lifted her onto his knee, and brought both his arms close about her. Her head was on his shoulder.

Presently he stirred and said, half-laughing. 'I swore this must never happen.'

'Do you regret it?'

'No.' Fervently. 'But it's deuced awkward, all the same.'

'Oh, this terrible secret of yours! Tell me now!'

He laughed again, but without mirth. 'I wonder if I dare. I wonder if you will box my ears when you hear it, and turn me out of doors!'

'Why should I? I swear...'

'Don't swear!' He laid his finger on her lips, and she kissed it, which made him shake his head, and snatch her up into his arms and kiss her all over again. This time there was nothing tender about the kiss, and yet she was not afraid. She wanted it to go on for ever, but he seemed to be fighting a battle with himself, breathing hard, his hands holding her fast, but no longer close to him. She opened her eyes, to see that he had closed his. He looked as if he were in pain.

Suddenly he tipped her onto the seat, and stood up, straightening his lace-edged cravat.

She felt soft and warm, and loving. She said, 'I think I love you, Robin.'

'Do you only "think" it? Now I "know" that I love you, and always will.'

'In spite of my wilfulness, and my poverty?'

'Perhaps because of it. Perhaps because

you are unlike anything I have ever known. Perhaps I have always loved you ... ever since I first saw you as a child ... so brave, riding my great horse ... so kind when I was sick at heart. Perhaps that was why I could never take to any of the girls I met later.'

'Do you wish me to say that I've always loved you, too? Well, perhaps I have, for it's true that I never favoured any but men of your build and colouring. Is your hair still fair, beneath the powder?'

'Yes, but ... what of Sir Maurice? You favoured him, even though...'

'Do you know anything to his discredit?' She frowned, and glanced over her shoulder. How could she now prevent Maurice from bursting in on her?

'I know little to his credit,' said Robin slowly. 'I am trying to discount my jealousy, you understand. But I know that he has moved in with a fellow gambler locally, and that he has drawn the young Hartley boys into his toils. I'm told that a small fortune has changed hands this last week, which may be one reason why Sir Maurice smiles so much.'

She bit her lip. 'The Hartley boys are foolish if they can't see for themselves what kind of man he is. But what can I do about it? Nothing.'

'You could send the man packing.'

'You really are jealous of him, aren't you?'

'What right have I to be jealous?' Yet his hands clenched at his sides. 'Elisabeth, are you playing with me again?'

'Perhaps I am.' She was finding it hard to concentrate on what he was saying. Sir Maurice must have been at large in the Hall for some considerable time. How was she to protect Robin, who was all unsuspicious of danger?

She said, 'I think we should go back to the house. I believe we should speak together in private…'

'Are we not private here?'

It was too late. Into the garden came Sir Maurice, looking triumphant, and behind him came his groom, an ostler from the stables and her own footman. They flanked that representative of law and order, the village beadle.

'Arrest that man!' said Sir Maurice, pointing to Robin.

EIGHT

'What the devil?' Robin looked more surprised than frightened.

The beadle looked uncomfortable, but stepped forward and laid his hand on Robin's shoulder. 'I arrest you, sir, in the name of the King!'

Robin said, 'Has the world gone mad?'

'No, sir,' said the beadle stolidly. 'We found them pictures with the diamonds on them, in your saddlebags. So if you'll come along with me now, quietly...? No need to distress the lady.'

Robin took a step back. 'The miniatures? But this is ridiculous! They are mine, and I can prove it.'

'You will have every chance to present your defence in court at the next Assizes,' said Sir Maurice. 'Beadle, take the man away and lock him up. Best set his legs in irons, for he's a slippery rogue, I fear.'

Robin stood fast when the beadle laid a heavy hand on his shoulder, and tried to lead him away.

'Come along now,' said the beadle, raising his stick in half-hearted manner. 'You don't want me to knock you out, in front of the lady, do you?'

Robin turned to Elisabeth. 'For God's sake, Elisabeth! I can explain…'

'Don't look to her for help,' said Sir Maurice, smiling widely. 'She's been fully aware of everything we've done, from the beginning. It was she who reported that the miniatures were missing in the first place, and it was she who held you in conversation this morning till we were able to search your bags.'

Robin put a hand to his head, and then plunged into his pocket to retrieve the note Sir Maurice had written to Elisabeth that morning. He read it once, and then read it through again.

Elisabeth seemed unable to speak or to move. She felt as if she were about to shatter into a thousand pieces of fragile glass … the shock of discovering that Robin was indeed a thief … that he had deceived her all along … it was too much.

Robin looked at her. He was still holding the note in his hands. Now he held it out to her, begging her to repudiate it.

Sir Maurice went to stand behind Elisabeth, who was still sitting on the bench. He put his hand on her shoulder, claiming ownership.

'Didn't she fool you prettily? Didn't she lead you on from folly to folly? I was stationed behind that half-open door there, and could hear everything. I could have intervened at any time after the miniatures were recovered, of course, but it amused me to see how far she would lead you on.'

Robin went white. His face looked like that of a dead man. Even his brilliant eyes seemed to lose their lustre and looked like pebbles of grey stone.

'I see that I must put you out of your misery,' said Sir Maurice, caressing Elisabeth's shoulder. 'The lady's fortune has not been whittled away by speculation since her father died, in fact I believe it has rather increased in value. As for the palazzo in Rome, the apartment in Paris, and the house in London, all are in perfect order, fully staffed, and likely to remain so.'

Robin made a movement with his hands, as if trying to push away this knowledge, but Sir Maurice continued.

'Did you really think that you, a penniless, nameless farmer, could woo the Lady Elisabeth Silverwood?'

Robin flushed an angry red, and then the colour receded from his face, leaving it grey and drawn.

'Well?' enquired Sir Maurice. 'How does it feel to be so thoroughly fooled?'

Robin stared at Sir Maurice, but it seemed unlikely that he saw him clearly. The beadle touched Robin on the shoulder again. Robin shook off the beadle's arm, and walked ahead of him, out of the garden. He did not look back.

At a nod from Sir Maurice, the other servants also faded away.

Sir Maurice sighed. 'Well, a good morning's work, wouldn't you agree? And now, my little love...' He sat beside Elisabeth, and put his arm about her.

She got to her feet with a convulsive movement. 'I ... forgive me, but I am not well.'

Her head felt as if it were bursting, and she could not breathe ... she was so tightly laced that she could not get enough air into her lungs ... she had never fainted in her life before, but now the sky was darkening about her, and the earth was coming up to meet her...

A doctor was called, and diagnosed a slight fever, caught on one of Elisabeth's imprudent expeditions to the village. He prescribed certain noxious remedies for the patient, which left Elisabeth hardly able to lift her hand from the sheet for weakness.

She lay without speaking, staring up at the tester. She accepted the broth and the bread and milk which they brought her, and gradually her body began to recover its strength.

It seemed however, that her mind had received too great a shock for her to be moved to Bath straight away.

After some days she was carried downstairs by the footman, to rest in the library for a few hours. She was still very weak and prone to tears.

She had told her aunt that she wished to see no visitors for the moment, but no amount of telling would convince Mrs Marriott that this included Sir Maurice. He haunted the house, bearing gifts of hot-house flowers, fruit and wine for the invalid.

She did not wish to see him, and she told him so. He disregarded her statement as the vapourings of an invalid, and continued to call. She told the footman to deny Sir Maurice entry, but was not surprised when this instruction, too was disregarded. She could keep Sir Maurice at bay no longer. She was beaten, and they both knew it. There could be but one end to his wooing now that Robin had been removed from the scene.

No one had mentioned Robin's name to her since his arrest. Yet after the first shock, Elisabeth found herself consumed with regret ... and also with shame. She had not intended to betray him, but she had in fact done so.

It no longer seemed to matter that he had deserved everything he had got. She felt that she was, perhaps, equally guilty. The look on his face when Sir Maurice had laughed at him ... it haunted her, day and night.

Her spirits were like lead, and nothing seemed able to lift her depression. The doctor told her it was a natural result of her bout of fever, but she knew it was not.

One afternoon, when she had been tucked up to rest in the library for some time, Sir Maurice arrived. He was wearing a new apple-green brocade coat with deep cuffs, and his silk waistcoat was smothered with brilliant embroidery. He looked magnificent.

She allowed him to lift her hand to his lips, and nodded when he begged permission to sit beside her. The first sight of him dressed in new clothes, told her the reason for this particular visit. They both knew that he was closing in for the kill.

'You have had no other callers as yet?' he asked.

She shook her head. She wished her aunt had seen fit to stay in the room, but she knew her wish was a vain one.

Sir Maurice had retained her hand in his, and now proceeded to play with her fingers.

'What a pretty little hand it is,' he said, 'And matches its owner to perfection.'

She let her hand fall back against the chair. She had heard compliments like that every day for years, and no longer valued them. There had only been one man in her life who paid her compliments as if they came from the heart ... and he was a proven thief and liar...

So she sighed, and said that Sir Maurice

was too good, to spend so much time with a creature such as herself, who was so low in spirits.

'You undertook too much,' said Sir Maurice. 'You would not listen to advice. You overtaxed your strength, apeing the man...'

'On the estate, you mean? Yes, perhaps.' But she had not thought so at the time. She had felt so full of energy, and ideas when riding about with Robin, and discussing repairs and improvements ... ah, Robin ... false Robin...

'I shall not allow you to do so again,' he said, assuming ownership. 'I can't have you jeopardising your strength by doing a clerk's work.'

She had no strength to fight. She said, 'Perhaps you are right.'

'I'm sure that I'm right. You must put all thoughts of the estate out of your pretty little head. There is absolutely no need for you to trouble yourself with it again. Is that clear?'

She made a restless movement. 'I've no steward here, now.'

'I'll appoint a man. You can trust me to see that your interests are well served, because they are my interests also ... aren't they?'

'Very well,' she said. Of course he would appoint a man after his own mind, a man who would take the maximum out of the estate. Sir Maurice had expensive tastes, and she was under no illusion as to what would happen to her fortune when he laid his hands on it.

He laid his large white hand on her shoulder, and leaned forward to kiss her lips. Deep inside her something seemed to rebel. She sobbed aloud, and closed her eyes on painful tears.

'My dear!' He had his arm about her. But he continued to smile, and she knew that he was aware why she cried, and was amused.

'I cannot help it,' she said, trying to stifle her sobs. 'I am very weak, still.'

'Yes, yes. As soon as you are fit to travel, I'll take you to Bath to recover your strength. You approve of Bath, don't you?'

'Yes, I'd like to leave here as soon as possible. Everything reminds me of...'

'...of your little folly? Yes, of course it does.' He was definitely amused, but also perhaps a little annoyed. The skin about his nostrils looked pinched, even though he continued to smile. 'You must look to the future now, my dear. Perhaps you should order some new clothes from London for our nuptials. We must hold some sort of reception here on the day, of course. We shall invite the man I'm staying with, and the Hartleys, also. Then there are several neighbours who've been assiduous in calling of late. I suppose the curate and the doctor will expect an invitation as well. Is there anyone else?'

She wanted to ask about Robin, but could not. She tried to smile, and he took that as consent for his plans.

'I think, my dear, that you should tell your maid to powder your hair again, as you used to do in town. Or perhaps we should send for a good barber from Warwick, who knows how to create an impressive coiffure? It will never do for you to drop into the ways of the country bumpkin, just because you have been ill for a few days. I will send for some French perfumes for you, and with some powder and paint, perhaps a patch or two, you'll soon look the modish lady once again.'

'Yes, I suppose I have allowed myself to lapse into country ways.'

'Then, shall I arrange everything for this coming Sunday?'

She started, and did not reply. Suddenly she realised that it was raining hard, and that the wind was blowing across the chimney tops, making a wailing noise. The keening sound echoed in her heart.

Sir Maurice said, 'The Hartleys know of a chaplain ... a friend of theirs hereabouts keeps one to tutor his children. We will set your aunt to work with the housekeeper, to bake some sort of wedding feast, shall we?'

'Sunday? But that's very soon, isn't it? I thought ... I must write to Mr Deeds, my man of business. There must be a marriage settlement drawn up between us.'

141

A marriage settlement would ensure that Sir Maurice could not squander all her fortune at the gaming tables, and would reserve sufficient funds to enable their children to be brought up decently. It would also provide her with a sum for dress, so that she need not beg him for money at every turn.

'Oh, we can't wait for Mr Deeds,' said Sir Maurice, with a smile. 'He may take months to prepare his documents, and I certainly can't wait that long. I want to take you to Bath as soon as we are wed.'

'We could be wed in Bath, perhaps.'

'Certainly not!' He kissed her again, and this time she closed her eyes and stiffened, but did not weep. The time for tears was past. Her one and only romance had shown her the folly of stepping out of her world. Life must go on.

'Then we are agreed?' he said.

She sighed. She supposed there was no help for it, but to marry him. It would not be a bad life, if only she could put all thoughts of Robin out of her head. But first she must learn what had become of him.

'What has become of … that man … the one who wronged me?'

Sir Maurice became very still. 'He's well enough, I assume.'

'Do you not know?'

'Why, I see no need to enquire daily as to his health. He was safely locked up in the village jail, I suppose.'

The village pound or jail was usually required to house stray animals, not men. Perhaps the occasional drunk might be put there overnight till he had sobered up. The stone-built pound was primitive, to say the least. There was one small barred unglazed window, and a low door.

She shuddered. 'How long is it since he was put in there? I've lost count of the days since I've been ill.'

'Four days, I suppose.'

'Four days and nights in that terrible place?'

'Naturally he would have been taken before a magistrate and removed to Warwick jail long before this, but Squire Hartley's away from home. Only a magistrate can commit him to jail.'

'Let him go, Sir Maurice. You've recovered the miniatures, destroyed his pride and his good name, and seen him dismissed from his job. Isn't that enough?'

'My dear, are you still enchanted by that young man?'

'No.' Violently. 'But I think he's been punished enough.'

'I don't. The man dared to raise his eyes to you...'

'...only because I encouraged him to do so. Yes, if blame there must be, then let me take my share of it. He'd never have said

143

anything, if I'd not flirted with him.'

'Was it only a flirtation?' wondered Sir Maurice.

'What else?' said Elisabeth, with her chin in the air. 'He hinted at a secret in his past... I was perhaps a little bored ... and intrigued. He was the handsomest man I had seen in the country ... and so I flirted with him.'

He pinched her fingers. 'You'll not flirt with anyone else, Elisabeth. Take my word for it, when you are my wife, you will not flirt with anyone else ... but me.'

'Probably not,' she said, between her teeth. 'I have lost the taste for it, entirely, since...' Her voice trailed away. She was shocked to find herself still so close to tears.

She said, 'I beg of you to let the man go.'

'If you'll kiss me for it, my dear. I'll consider it. I want you to come to me willingly, you know. I'd like you to prove to me, by kissing me, that you have completely put that young man out of your mind.'

'Oh, I assure you, I have.' She lifted her face for his kiss, trying not to think of Robin's dear face ... deceitful face...

Sir Maurice was smiling as he bent over her. His mouth covered hers, and she felt as if he were trying to draw the very life out of her body, like a leech. His hands worked their way over her low-cut dress, to fasten on her shoulders – to take possession of her.

If only she could get the memory of another man's kisses out of her mind. She wanted to forget Robin, with all her heart. She must, she would try to love Sir Maurice instead.

'Well, well!' Sir Maurice stood back, re-settling the lace of his cravat. He looked pleased with himself. 'So it seems there is still some fire in your veins, my dear! I can hardly wait for our wedding night.'

She had thought of Robin, when she had kissed Sir Maurice. Momentarily she closed her eyes, dreading lest he discover her secret.

She said, 'Now, Sir Maurice, ring the bell and give orders to release your prisoner.'

Sir Maurice's lips drew back from his teeth into an extremely unpleasant version of his usual wide smile. 'Not so fast, my dear. I said that I'd consider that matter of his release if you kissed me, and I will consider it – at leisure. There is, perhaps, something to be said for letting the man go, without bringing him to trial. For instance, it would expose you to ridicule, if he were brought to trial. He fooled you very neatly, didn't he? Yes, there is that. But on the other hand, I'm inclined to let the matter take its course, to prove that we will not tolerate theft.'

She gripped the arms of her chair. 'But if it comes to a trial and he is convicted…'

'…doubtless he'll be transported for life to

the colonies. Heigh-ho, the way of the trans-gressor is hard, isn't it?'

'Do I have to go on my knees and beg?' There was a break in her voice, despite her best efforts.

'My dear, I'd do anything to serve you ... and I think I would be serving you best by letting the young man stand trial in the usual way. Now, let us summon your aunt and the housekeeper to hear the good news of our betrothal. No doubt they'll be over-joyed. We must instruct the housekeeper to issue extra rations of ale to the servants, so that they may celebrate ... and perhaps when I pass back through the village, I'll tell the innkeeper to serve free drinks all round in your honour. Doubtless the news will spread rapidly.'

He meant that Robin would hear of it tonight, where he lay in leg irons, in the pound. She turned her head away, and fought to control herself.

Mrs Marriott came, and the housekeeper, and Sir Maurice made his announcement, which appeared to be not unexpected. Elisabeth smiled and smiled, and left all the talking to Sir Maurice. She longed for him to go. She suggested that he ought to make sure of securing the chaplain for Sunday, and to her relief he went away to do so.

She looked up at the portrait of Sir Wil-liam, and wondered what he thought of the situation. If he had lived ... if he had not left all his money to Elisabeth ... if she had never taken it into her head to visit Denys Hall ... had never seen Robin...

Difficult tears slid down her cheeks, and were wiped away. She must think. Robin might deserve punishment, but he did not deserve to be transported for life to Australia. She must do something to help him. But what?

Well, she could send for the beadle, and order him to release Robin.

No, that would not do, for Sir Maurice would be told as soon as she gave an order to one of the servants that she wished to see the beadle. She suspected that even if her footman had not been in Sir Maurice's pay when they left London, he was certainly so now. There was no mistaking the glances of complicity which passed between Sir Maurice and the footman when they were in the same room. Just now, for instance, when the bell had been rung for the housekeeper, and the footman had arrived as if by magic, within seconds ... he must have been listening outside the door...

She ought to have dismissed the man weeks ago, but it had not seemed important ... until now.

Well, she must go herself into the village, as soon as she could ride. She threw aside her wraps and stood, balancing herself against the back of the chair. Her knees felt like cotton, and her arms like lead, but she persevered. She walked across to the library table, and back. And again.

Perhaps by tomorrow evening she would be fit enough to mount a horse. But by tomorrow evening, Robin would have been in that dreadful place, with his legs fast in irons, for five days and nights.

She glanced out of the window. It was still sleeting, and the fire in the library only made the cold weather outside more uninviting. The thought of Robin sitting in that cold, dank stone jail set her in motion again. She walked across to the window and back, touching the bookcases now and then to keep her balance.

And again.

She rested a while, and got to her feet again. She must, she would ride into the village on the morrow. Every time she stopped to rest, she looked up at the portrait of Sir William in silent accusation. It was all his fault…

The fierce grey eyes looked down at her as if to say, Whose fault, Elisabeth? If he betrayed you, did you not also betray him?

By the following afternoon the Lady Elisabeth said she felt so much recovered from her recent indisposition that she would ride out in the Park for a while. She over-ruled her aunt's protests, ordered her horse to be brought round, and with her groom behind, gently trotted down into the village. The rain had stopped, and it was a lovely afternoon.

She had not been that way for over a week, and everywhere there was a bustle of workmen. The children seemed less listless, the women at the doorways curtsied when they saw her coming, and some of them even smiled at her.

She bowed and smiled back, and all the time she was thinking that she did not deserve their good opinion of her. It was Robin's energy and foresight which had improved their living conditions.

She wondered if Sir Maurice would stop all work on the village when they were married, and thought that he might well do so. He thought too much meat in peasants' bellies brought about revolution.

She walked her horse across the village green. There stood the most prosperous building in the place, the inn. Beside the inn, and a little to one side, crouched the ugly stone beehive of the village pound.

She could not look. But she must do so.

Her hands jerked her horse to a standstill, for the door of the pound gaped wide, and it was clear that it contained nothing but a heap of dirty straw.

NINE

There was a mounting block by the inn. With her groom's assistance she dismounted from her horse. She was trembling, and was only too glad to sit on the bench nearby. She sent a lad for the beadle and told her groom to walk the horses for a while.

'My lady?' The beadle tugged at his forelock, and made a leg.

'Your prisoner.' She gestured towards the pound with her riding crop. 'Has he escaped?' The thought made her heart beat faster.

'Why, no. He was never put in there, my lady.'

'Explain yourself, sirrah!' Anxiety made her sharp.'

'Why, when he left the Hall he stopped and said he wanted to see the warrant for his arrest, but I had none as Sir Maurice had not had time to get it. Then the gentleman said he thought Squire Hartley was the nearest magistrate, and suggested that we went direct to him, instead of coming here to the pound first. For you must know, my lady, that the pound is not suitable to house gentry.'

'Indeed, no,' said Elisabeth. She put one hand to her side. Was Robin already in Warwick prison? 'Continue. You went direct to Squire Hartley's place, and then…?'

'The Squire saw us straight away. Mr Prior asked if he might have a word in private with the Squire, and so I waited outside the door awhile. Then the Squire came out and sent me back to the Hall with a note for your housekeeper. When I got back with her reply, the Squire told me I was not needed any more, for he was taking Mr Prior into Warwick himself. I saw them get into the Squire's chaise and off they went, within the hour. And that is the last I seen of either of them, my lady.'

So, Robin was in Warwick prison, and her great effort on his behalf had been in vain. She could never get him out of Warwick prison. He would have to stand his trial, and would surely be convicted and…

She forced the black cloud away, and presently found she could breathe more easily.

'Will that be all, my lady?'

She nodded, he made a leg, and went away.

What was she to do now? Perhaps she could go on to the Squire's, and explain to him that she did not wish to prosecute? The miniatures had been recovered, and she had no wish for publicity. Yes, that was what she must do … but not today, for she still felt sick and faint.

First, she must get back to the Hall, and rest.

Then it occurred to her that Sir Maurice must pass through the village every day on his way to visit her, and must have noticed that the pound was empty. Had he played on her ignorance, to get her to kiss him?

She was too tired to change out of her riding clothes when she got back to the Hall, and in spite of her maid's protests, fell into the big chair in the Library, just as she was.

The word 'never' was going through her head, over and over again. She would never see Robin again, if he were not rescued soon. She slid into sleep, and the word 'never' went with her. She woke with the word still ringing in her ears, and tears running down her cheeks.

And then, as clearly as if he had been standing over her, she heard old Sir William say, 'I never want to hear his name mentioned again!'

She opened her eyes and sat upright, for in fact Sir William had indeed spoken those words in her hearing, and he had been speaking about Robin. She could see herself as a child standing here in the library with her hand in her father's ... and Sir William, his face purple with rage, standing with his back to the fire, saying, 'I never want to hear his name mentioned again!'

Another memory, even sharper in detail, came into focus. She was running along the Gallery upstairs trying to catch up with Robin, who was leaving the Hall for ever. He dropped the saddle bags he was carrying, and lifted her up in his arms.

She had been crying. 'They said you were leaving, and that I'd never see you again!'

Robin said, 'Perhaps I'll come back one day ... and then you'll be grown-up, and won't know me...'

Elisabeth sat on beside the fire, trying to remember.

She rather thought she had kissed him then and there in the Long Gallery. He had been wearing an olive green coat ... booted and spurred for his journey ... his fair hair tied back with a ribbon...

She closed her eyes. It was no good. She could recall no more. Excitement began to work within her, for she scented a mystery in the past.

Her mind ranged over various possibilities, and fastened on the two miniatures. Slowly she made her way into the parlour, where they hung by the fireplace. The set was complete again, for Sir Maurice had replaced the two which Robin had taken, in their old places.

She lifted them off their nails, and took them to the window. One was of a man in a dark red coat, and now that she looked more closely, she could see that despite the shape of the old-fashioned wig which he wore, there was a resemblance to Robin. The other was a copy of a portrait which hung in the Gallery upstairs, and if she remembered aright, he had been some brother or cousin of old Sir William's.

Neither of the miniatures bore any superscription on the back, to identify the sitter.

Soon Elisabeth's maid came to assist her mistress out of the riding habit and tight corset, and into a loose-bodied saque of flowing pink silk. Elisabeth chose to dine by the fire in her bedroom, but afterwards summoned the housekeeper to attend her in the Long Gallery.

The portrait which interested her so much was of a hard-faced man in a periwig which dated back to the turn of the century. He was richly dressed. The portrait was indifferently well painted, and probably not valuable, yet Sir William or someone else in the family had thought it worth while to have it copied in miniature.

The housekeeper came, and bobbed a curtsey.

'I am interested in this portrait,' said Elisabeth. 'Were you here at the Hall in this man's time?'

'Yes, my lady. Or rather, I saw the gentleman once or twice when I was a little girl, but he died before I came to work here. He was Sir William's brother that lost a fortune at the gaming tables and died young, of a broken heart, they say.'

'Was his heart broken by a woman?'

The housekeeper hesitated. 'I did hear he treated his wife badly, and that he'd only married her for her money. They said he could have born the loss of his wife and child better than the loss of his fortune... He quarrelled with Sir William over his debts, took to his bed and died. I think Sir William was sorry, after, for when his sister-in-law died, he took the boy in and brought him up as his own.'

'You remember the nephew, then?'

'Yes, my lady. He was a wild one, made for any adventure. There was no real vice in him, I believe, but Sir William had never been one to make allowances, and there were frequent quarrels. The young master would go off and stay with one of his young friends for weeks, sometimes, waiting for Sir William to get over his bad temper. Then one day we heard he'd got a farmer's daughter into trouble, and that was the end of him.'

'There was a scandal?'

'Yes, my lady. I'd left the Hall by then, to marry, but of course we all heard about it. The young master came back once, trying to see Sir William, but the old man turned him away.'

Elisabeth gazed at the portrait. 'Am I dreaming, or is there a resemblance between this man and Mr Prior?'

The housekeeper looked uncomfortable. 'My lady, I'd never have mentioned, but … yes.'

'You believe that Mr Prior was the natural son of Sir William's nephew? Yes, so do I. What did you think of Mr Prior?'

'He treated us well, my lady. We were all very sorry to hear about … about his trouble.'

Elisabeth sighed, and dismissed the woman. She retired to her room, for she was still feeling weak.

So, the mystery was solved, at last. Robin had declared that he was legitimate out of shame, perhaps … or perhaps he had lied about that … or possibly his father had actually married the Prior girl after their child was born. Under the laws of that day, such a late marriage would not have made the child legitimate.

Robin might under such circumstances feel that he had some sort of claim – in a twisted way – to the miniatures of his father and grandfather, and had taken them, intending to tell Elisabeth later what he had done.

She could understand why he had not wished to tell her of his questionable parentage while he was working for her, and living under the roof of his forefathers.

She could sympathise with Robin, even though she could not condone his crime. Whatever happened, she must see to it that he did not stand trial. She would send a note to Squire Hartley on the morrow, asking him to call upon her.

The door opened, and Sir Maurice walked into her bedroom. He was smiling, and very sure of himself.

Elisabeth rose in a panic. He had never intruded into her bedroom before, and it had never occurred to her that he would. She reached for the bell-pull, but he forestalled her with a hand on her arm.

'Sir Maurice! This is outrageous!'

'My dear, it is very natural. I heard you were so unwise as to ride down into the village today...'

'How did you hear? By my footman, I suppose? I will dismiss the man at once!'

'Let us say that I have friends in your household. And why not? Are we not shortly to become one household? Naturally I wished to assure myself that my betrothed had suffered no hurt...'

'I'm well enough. Release me. I wish to summon my maid ... my aunt...'

'Your aunt and I have a pretty good understanding, I believe.'

Elisabeth's colour had risen, and her fingers trembled as he took them in his clasp.

He said, 'As I suspected, you have over-exerted yourself. I see I must take a high hand with you, and forbid you to leave the house for the present.'

'It did me good to ride out for a short while. I was stifling inside the house.'

'...and curious about our young friend?'

'Yes, that as well.' She tried to put a bold front on it. 'You did not tell me that he had been taken to Warwick already.'

'Did I not?' The man was playing with her.

He bent low, so low that his breath was warm on her shoulder. She shrank from him, despite her intention to appear indifferent.

He smiled, widely. 'It seems to me that you are over-concerned with our young thief.'

'Has it occurred to you that Robin Prior might feel he had some right to the miniatures?'

Sir Maurice inspected his fingernails, and took a seat on the far side of the fireplace.

'You do not answer, Sir Maurice.' She held onto her temper with difficulty.

'You mean that our ne-er-do-well might be a by-blow of the quarrelsome and extensive Denys family? Yes, it had occurred to me. That does not, of course, excuse the theft.'

'It does, perhaps, make it understandable. Sir Maurice, I tell you plainly that I will not prosecute.'

'You have no choice, my dear. The matter is

159

now, happily, out of our hands. I must admit that when I first discovered the pound was empty, I was somewhat disturbed. Thoughts of calling in the Bow Street Runners flitted through my mind. But then I heard that the thief had actually put his head into the lion's mouth of his own accord ... had actually gone to Squire Hartley himself, and given himself up...!' Sir Maurice laughed.

Elisabeth's hands clenched on the arms of her chair.

Sir Maurice said, 'He couldn't have approached a magistrate more to my liking, could he? The young Hartley boys have been playing deep at cards and I hold a good many of their IOU's. Naturally the father would not wish to offend me in any way. But I made assurance doubly sure by sending the Squire a formal letter accusing the man Prior of theft. As a magistrate, he must act upon such complaints. I think we can now put the case out of our minds.'

'Suppose that I were to go to Squire Hartley myself, and intervene...'

'It would do no good. The rogue has by now been formally charged and committed to jail. He will have to stand trial in due course.'

Elisabeth turned her head away, that he might not see the tears of weakness in her eyes. She said, 'I must bid you goodnight, Sir Maurice. I'm still not fully recovered, and I wish to retire early.'

'So you should, my dear.' He did not go, but leaned forward in his chair, to put his hand on her knee. 'And no more nonsense about leaving the house without my escort. I've settled with your aunt that we are to be wed the day after tomorrow, and I've laid on the chaplain accordingly.'

'So soon?'

'Why not? The villagers are delighted, for I've given orders for an ox to be killed and roasted whole on the village green. They'll have plenty of ale to drink, and are anticipating the feast with glee. The day after the ceremony we will be off to Bath.'

'I am not well enough to travel as yet.'

'If you were well enough to ride down to the village today, you will be well enough to travel in my chaise in three days' time. Let us have no more nonsense, Elisabeth. In future you will be governed by me in all things. Do you understand?'

'I don't want to marry a man who will thwart me at every turn.'

'You may not wish it,' and here he smiled again, 'But that is what will happen. I'm sure one of your die-away lovers, Elisabeth. I intend to be master of our house, in every way. Do you understand?'

Looking into his eyes she realised that he knew how she felt about him, and did not care. In fact, it seemed to amuse him.

'Leave me!' she said. 'And pray do not enter my rooms again without permission.'

'I'll do as I think fit. You've given me the right to enter your rooms whenever I wish, and I intend to take every advantage of my position.'

'Not till we're wed! You wouldn't like it if I screamed for help, and the servants were to gossip in the village … and to our neighbours…'

He drew back. For a moment she had him at a disadvantage.

'Well, well,' he said. 'So she still has a sting in her tongue? I thought I had you tamed, my dear. But never fear, it will not be long till I have you safe in my hands … forever … and no-one in heaven or hell will come between us then.'

He was still smiling, but there was an ugly gleam in his eyes.

Early the following morning Elisabeth went to her aunt's room. Mrs Marriott was sitting up in bed wearing an enormous beribboned cap, and drinking chocolate.

'So, my dear! The last day of your freedom!'

'I suppose so, but I didn't come to talk about that. Aunt, I asked you never to leave me alone with Sir Maurice…'

Mrs Marriott wagged a finger at her niece. 'I knew better than to heed you, my love.

Why, if I'd played the chaperone, I daresay you'd still be without a husband in sight.'

'Let me speak plainly. I want to know how much he has paid for your services?'

A little natural colour tinged Mrs Marriott's rouged cheeks. 'What a dreadful thing to say! How ungrateful!' She fished for her handkerchief.

Elisabeth snatched the handkerchief from her aunt, and held it out of reach. 'Tell me what I want to know, or I'll empty the contents of your water jug on you as you lie in bed!'

'Why, I don't have the slightest idea what you mean...'

Then as Elisabeth seized the jug and brought it over to the bed, Mrs Marriott gave a little scream, and cowered under the sheets. 'My dear, have mercy! Heavens, such a termagent! It's more than time you were tamed, as Sir Maurice says!'

She screamed again as the first drops of water splashed on to her shoulder, and cried again for mercy.

'Tell me!' said Elisabeth, between her teeth.

'He said ... he promised ... indeed, Elisabeth, it is not right for you to torture me ... a small pension he promised me, that was all. Just enough for me to retire to Bath in lodgings, where there is so much to make life enjoyable ... oh, my heart! Give me my smelling salts!'

Elisabeth threw her aunt the smelling salts, replaced the jug on the stand, and went downstairs with rebellion in her heart.

Her aunt's favours had been bought ... the footman had been bribed ... possibly at least one of the grooms was also in Sir Maurice's pay, to judge by the ease with which messages passed between them.

He knew all her movements within hours. Whatever she did today, he would know before nightfall. And in any case, he had forbidden her to leave the house without him.

She could have screamed with vexation, but that would only waste time, and she had so little time left. She paced up and down the library, biting her lip. How to escape, that was the question ... and where could she go ... and if she left the Hall unobtrusively with the help of servants who were still true to her ... but which of them were still true?

Presently the footman came to her.

'Squire Hartley has called, my lady. He said he did not know if you felt sufficiently recovered to see him on a small matter of business, but if not he would ask your permission to inspect the miniatures and certain papers in the secretaire. He was very forceful, my lady, and pushed past me into the parlour. Shall I send for the grooms, to show him out?'

'A matter of business?' she said. She thought, Robin!

'Yes, my lady. Shall I send word to Sir Maurice?'

'No, certainly not. I will see him myself.'

The man did not go. 'My lady, I believe Sir Maurice would not wish you to see this man.'

She stared. 'Why ever not? Open the doors for me, fellow!'

Still the man did not stand aside from the doors. She began to wonder, uneasily, if he meant to hold her in the library by force, and whether she ought to scream ... and if she did scream, whether anyone would pay the slightest attention or not.

He said, 'I should perhaps mention that there is someone with the Squire.'

'Well, who is it?'

'It is Mr Prior, my lady.'

TEN

Elisabeth put out her hand to steady herself, then walked up to the doors, and waited for the footman to throw them open for her. After a moment's hesitation, he did so, and she passed through. The man crossed the hall at her heels, stepped in front of her to open the parlour door, and closed it behind her.

The first person she saw was Robin, seated at the secretaire, but it was the Squire who came forward to greet her.

Squire Hartley had been standing by the fireplace, leaning forward to study the miniatures. He held out both hands to her in greeting, and said that he was glad to hear she was now fully recovered from her indisposition.

Robin had not risen when she came in, but when she extended her hand to him, and spoke his name, he rose to make her a formal bow. He did not look at her, or speak, and returned immediately to his examination of some papers which he had withdrawn from the desk.

He was wearing a new coat of olive green brocade embroidered in gold. There was a paler green silk waistcoat beneath, embroidered with fur and dark green leaves. His linen was faultless as ever, and there was more lace at his throat and on his cuffs than usual. His hair gleamed gold, and was free of powder.

He looked extremely elegant.

He did not look as if he had recently been languishing in jail.

Elisabeth sank into a nearby chair, and with her eyes still on Robin, asked the Squire what she might do for him.

'Well, my lady, it is just a formality, but we have to go into these matters thoroughly when a complaint has been laid.'

'I laid no complaint,' said Elisabeth, in a breathless voice. 'I don't wish to prosecute.'

The Squire said, 'We would not have intruded, but we thought it best to check for ourselves through the family papers. I believe you are without a man of business here at the moment, or we'd have asked for him.'

Elisabeth tried to give her attention to the Squire, while being aware of every movement that Robin made. Oh, if only he would look up and smile at her!

'Here's the second receipt,' said Robin, holding up a tattered piece of paper. He took it to the Squire, without glancing in Elisabeth's direction. She might as well not have existed, for all the notice he was taking of her.

'So it is,' said the Squire, in a pleased voice. He laid various papers out on a side-table, and glanced from one to another.

Elisabeth said, 'Gentlemen, if you would be so kind as to tell me...'

'My lady, would you say that this describes our two miniatures? Where is the reference? Ah, here it is. "A copy in miniature of the portrait of Francis Robert Denys, younger brother of Sir William Denys, in a frame wrought with the Denys arms on top." And the other reference is ... yes... "A miniature painted on ivory, in an oval frame set with nine diamonds, of Robert Francis Denys, in a red coat ... both miniatures at present hanging in the small parlour at Denys Hall.' To the best of your knowledge, does that describe the two miniatures which have caused all the trouble?'

'Yes,' said Elisabeth, 'but...'

The Squire raised his hand. 'And now, Robin; show me if you will, which of the miniatures were found in your possession last week.'

'That one and that,' said Robin, pointing to the miniatures he had taken.

'Ah,' said the Squire, with every evidence of satisfaction. He put up his papers in his coat pocket, and beamed at Elisabeth. 'A most satisfactory conclusion to what might have been a particularly nasty affair. I must thank you, my lady, for allowing us access to the miniatures once again … particularly on a day when you must have a thousand and one things to do… I shall of course be happy to attend your nuptials tomorrow with my dear wife and sons. I must say we are all looking forward to it.'

Robin handed the Squire a folded sheaf of papers. 'You are forgetting the inventory. You may need that.'

The Squire said to Elisabeth. 'You permit that I take it away with me for a few days?'

'I don't understand,' said Elisabeth. 'I want the case stopped.'

The Squire was soothing. 'I'll see that the papers are returned to the right people in due course. I believe you plan to remove to Bath?'

'I believe so,' said Elisabeth. She was swamped with misery. Robin was still avoiding her eye, and she did not know how she was going to bear it. Was he at liberty this morning in the custody of the Squire, and if so, why?

She stood up. 'Squire, I'd beg a favour of you.'

'Anything, my lady. You have but to ask.'

'I'd like five minutes conversation alone with … this gentleman.'

'But…' said the Squire.

'I see no reason for it,' said Robin, cutting across the Squire's objection.

'If you please!' cried Elisabeth, clasping

her hands together, 'It is a matter of the greatest importance!'

The Squire pursed his lips, looking from Robin's averted face to Elisabeth's eager one. 'Well,' he said, 'I'd a thought just now … perhaps I ought to consult with your housekeeper … so if you'll excuse me?'

Elisabeth urged him to the door. 'Send for wine … anything!'

She shut the door on the Squire, and set her back to it. Robin was looking at her with chilly dislike.

She said, 'Won't you forgive me? It wasn't my idea to charge you with theft. Indeed, I have been trying to get you released, but…'

'My lady!' He bowed slightly, turning her excuses aside as of no importance.

She bit her lip. 'Very well. I can understand how you feel, I suppose. But we are wasting time.' She ran to the window, and threw the casement wide. It would be a struggle for his broad shoulders to get through, but she thought he might manage it. 'Here, you can leave by the window and be far away by the time you are missed. I will keep the Squire occupied for as long as I can. You will need money… Here, take my rings … go abroad for a while. It will all be forgotten soon enough, and then you can return.'

She held out her rings, but he would not take them.

'But Robin, I can't bear it if you are transported to Australia for theft! Whatever you think of me – and I admit I did lie to you that day – only take the jewels and go!'

She could feel tears trickle down her cheeks, but he was unmoved.

'Tears, madam?' he said, in a hard voice. 'What an actress you would have made, to be sure!'

'I am not acting. Oh, how can I make you believe me?'

After a short pause he said, 'Do not distress yourself. I have a perfect defence to the charge you laid against me.'

'I laid no charge against you. I had nothing to do with it. It was all Sir Maurice's idea, and although I have begged and pleaded with him, he will not withdraw.'

'I daresay that after tomorrow you'll sing a different tune.'

'Do you think I want this marriage?' She dashed tears from her eyes. 'Believe me, I would escape from it if I could but...' She made a tired gesture of defeat. 'It is impossible.'

'You expect me to believe that, after what I saw and heard in the garden? When you had stationed him behind the door, to overhear what was said ... when you tricked and deceived me?'

'I didn't know he was there!' She wrung her hands in agony. 'Indeed I was not playing

172

with you. It's true I lied about losing my money, but I was so afraid for you … and I knew the miniatures were missing, and that you had a secret you would not tell me until you had left my employ … what was I to think, but that you were guilty in some way?'

He gave a hard laugh. 'I thank you for your trust in me!'

'But Robin, what else could I think? And when I discovered the truth…'

'What truth?'

'That your father ran off with a farmer's daughter … about the scandal … I can understand that you feel you belong to the Denys family, even though you have no legal right to the name. I do understand and in some way excuse what you did, taking the miniatures of your father and grandfather… But indeed it was not right!'

He was looking at her intently.

She laid her hands on his arm. 'I beg you, Robin, to believe me. I was shocked at first, I must confess, but I'd rather a thousand times listen to your words of love, than to those of Sir Maurice.'

'Yet you are marrying him tomorrow.'

'Yes … I wanted to wait at least until Marriage Settlements could be drawn up … but I was ill for a while … and you were in jail…'

'I heard about your illness only yesterday.' His voice was sharp. 'You are still pale. Did

173

you take a fever from your visits to the village?'

'The doctor seemed to think so, yes, but I'll be well enough soon, and I daresay I'll not be too unhappy. I understand Sir Maurice, even if I do not like him, and they say a wife should not expect too much in marriage.'

He put his arm about her, and guided her to a chair. It was the first time he had shown her any tenderness that day, and she was grateful for it. He knelt beside her, head bent, to chafe her hands. She wished he would look up, but he did not. Without powder and pomatum, his hair was inclined to go its own way over his ears, and at the nape of his neck. She longed to touch him, but dared not.

She said, 'Robin, believe me. I only want to help you.'

'How can I trust you, after what has happened?'

'Well, if I lied to you – and I admit that I did – yet you have lied to me as well.'

'My motive was a good one. I wished to spare you embarrassment.'

'And I lied to break down your pride … your stiff-necked Denys pride. Oh, Robin, could you not have told me the truth long ago?'

'Perhaps, but I didn't think so at the time. Elisabeth, I don't understand why you are marrying Sir Maurice.'

'Because he has bribed my servants, and my aunt, so that I cannot deny him entrance to the Hall. Because I am afraid what he can do to you.'

'I told you that you ought not to have been travelling around without the protection of a man.'

'It did not matter while my old steward was still able to travel with me, for he took care of everything. And while Sir William was alive, I was protected to some extent, for he controlled my fortune. But he died without appointing anyone to take over from him, or so Mr Deeds tells me. But it seems that I now have the right to dispose of myself and my property as I think best.'

'Your money ought to have been tied up in trust for life!' he sounded angry.

'Well, it was not, and I can do nothing about it now.'

'I would dispute that. If you were to come away with us now ... stay with the Hartleys, who would be glad to have you ... then Sir Maurice could not get at you, and you could send for Mr Deeds to make fresh disposition of your property.'

'Oh, I couldn't do that!'

'Why not?'

'You may not have heard, but the Hartleys are not to be trusted. Sir Maurice holds IOUs signed by the Hartley boys, and so the

Squire will deny him anything.'

'Elisabeth, this is not like you. You will not be married to a man you dislike purely because he wishes it? Where is your usual fire and courage?'

'Gone with the doctor's potions.' She tried to laugh, and almost made it. 'You are right, of course. I have allowed myself to fall into despair and there is no need for it. Perhaps I can still make a stand of sorts. After all, he can't drag me screaming to the altar, can he?'

He lifted his head, and looked her in the eye.

She caught her breath. His eyes were ice cold one moment, and the next they were warm with desire. She lifted her hand to touch his cheek, but let it fall again.

He said, 'Elisabeth, I made you an offer that day in the garden, and that offer still stands. If you love me, if you are not play-acting again, then you will come away with me, now. I will know how to take care of you.'

'What ... now? Through the window?'

'No, that is absurd. Come to me on neutral ground, and I will take you to safety, to one of my friends in Warwick. Or I will escort you to London, if you so wish.'

'I will not go to the Hartleys.'

'No, I understand, although you are mistaken in thinking Squire Hartley a puppet.

Come to me at the inn in the village…'

'But … how can that be? Are you able to escape from the Squire?'

'I am quite at liberty to move about as I please. I will be staying at the inn tonight, and will be there all day tomorrow, because I am expecting to meet some friends there.'

She bit her lip. 'Could I? I wonder!'

Now another fear presented itself to her. If Sir Maurice were to learn that Robin was at liberty, would there not be another demand for him to be arrested? And worse still, if Sir Maurice were to learn that Elisabeth were thinking of running away with Robin, would there not be a pursuit … and a duel … which could end only in Robin's death?

Elisabeth shuddered. She said, 'I will come to you, I promise, but only if you swear that you'll have a chaise ready, with good horses … if you'll promise me we may set off straight away, to France … Italy … anywhere.'

'But…'

'Yes, that's what I want,' she said, with a feverish air. 'I want you to take me on a honeymoon tour of Europe. I've money abroad, and we can go everywhere and see everything, and it will be wonderful.'

'Truly you are all sunshine and showers! What will you think of next?'

'You agree?'

'I suppose I must. When I'm with you, I

forget the good resolutions I have made. Common sense flies out of the window.'

'But you'll indulge me this one time?'

'I don't wish to marry you out of hand…'

'I wish it! It is so … so romantic!' He must never guess that the real reason for her haste lay in fear of what Sir Maurice would do, if he found out! Knowing Robin, he would be so stiff-necked as to refuse to run away, and then there would be a duel and … she shuddered.

'You are cold,' said Robin. He picked her up in his arms, and held her close.

She hid her face against his. 'You picked me up and held me like this once before … when we were young … do you remember? You were leaving the Hall, and I ran after you, crying…'

'And I kissed you … and you kissed me back … like this…'

She closed her eyes and put her hand up to the back of his neck, as his head bent to hers. It seemed probable that he only intended to kiss her lightly, for his lips barely touched hers before they began to withdraw. But then his arm moved further behind her shoulders, and his breath was hot upon her cheek.

'Elisabeth!' This time his lips came down hard on hers, and this time she could feel something of the passion that was running through him, in the sudden strength of his arms. The fire in his blood passed into hers, so that she strained up to meet him, both her arms about his neck ... feeling herself submerged in his strength, and fiercely glad that it should be so. She was being taken up and out of herself ... floating free...

And then, feeling slightly dizzy, she was conscious once more of being back on earth. She was still in his arms, but he had drawn back from her, breathing hard. She found she was breathing hard, too.

He put her down on her chair and almost ran away from her, to stand by the fireplace. He leaned his arms on the mantel, and rested his head on his arms.

She lay where he had left her, one hand to her heart, feeling the pleasure of that kiss still running through her body ... acting on her like a strong wine.

Someone scratched at the door, and Squire Hartley walked in. He was frowning. Robin jerked upright, and passed his hand back over his hair.

She sat upright, and tried to pretend that nothing had happened in the Squire's absence. 'You have finished interrogating my servants, I hope?'

'I merely wished to discover where the inventory had been kept recently, and who had done the job of checking it. Everything is pretty clear now, I think.' He addressed Robin. 'Shall we leave the lady to her preparations for the morrow?'

Robin bowed over her hand, and left the room. It seemed to take an earthquake to shake his composure, but once it was done, he did not recover quickly. Elisabeth liked that about him, too. It argued that his feelings ran deep.

She sat on in her chair, plotting and planning. Now that she had seen Robin again, she realised that she had been sliding into a dangerous situation.

What! Was she to be married off tomorrow merely because Sir Maurice wished for the match, and had a forceful way with him? Ridiculous!

Then a pang of fear shot through her. Well, if the worst came to the worst, she would run away to the inn ... and Robin ... and flee abroad...

She shook herself. This was absurd. She was no penniless cottage girl, but the mistress of a great establishment, with many servants at her beck and call, and many substantial neighbours within riding distance.

The Hartleys were her nearest neighbours on the east. To the west there were her own tenant farmers, who might or might not be able to stand up to Sir Maurice ... to the north was the Warwick road. Yes, she would take the Warwick road. The doctor lived that way, and so did an ancient lady who had called on her a week ago. The doctor might be in Sir Maurice's pay, of course … but the ancient dame could not be.

Elisabeth rang the bell, and ordered the footman to send to the stables for her mare to be saddled. The footman said, stolidly, that he feared Sir Maurice and the doctor would not approve.

'I don't give a fig for their approval!' flashed Elisabeth. 'Obey me instantly!'

The footman hesitated, and then went slowly away. Elisabeth rang for her maid, in order to change into her riding habit. The buxom maid who took this message looked scared and shortly after Mrs Marriott came in, followed by the lady's maid.

'Dearest!' Mrs Marriott smothered Elisabeth in a soft hug. 'You are distraught. You cannot possibly ride out today. You are not fit.'

'I am fit enough,' said Elisabeth, throwing off her aunt. 'And if that girl does not fetch me my riding things instantly, then she leaves this house within the hour!'

'Leave us,' said Mrs Marriott to the maid. The maid went out, looking apprehensive.

'Aunt,' said Elisabeth, between her teeth. 'This is no whim. I am in earnest. Who is the mistress of this household; you or I?'

'Sir Maurice will be here within the hour, my dear, and he will be highly displeased if he finds you've left the house without his knowledge.'

'He's not my husband yet … and indeed I begin to wonder if he ever will be!'

'You talk so wildly, dear! That proves you are not yet fully recovered. Sit down here, and I'll send for the doctor…'

'I don't need the doctor!'

'When Sir Maurice comes…'

'I don't wish to see him!'

Mrs Marriott paused. She looked distressed.

'Dearest, you are not wise. You are not yourself today, indeed you are not. You know very well it is not wise to cross Sir Maurice! Only recall that after tomorrow he'll have the right to restrict your comings and goings as much as he pleases…'

'All the more reason why I shouldn't marry him. Aunt, why do you take his part against me? Did you think I would cast you off without a penny when I married? Can you really trust a man such as Sir Maurice?'

'I trust him more than I'd trust a proven thief and liar. What sort of person would I be to allow you to throw yourself away on such a creature, eh? Tell me that! No, it is my duty to see you safely married to an eligible man, and Sir Maurice is everything that a man ought to be.'

'But I don't even like him!'

'You'll soon get over that, when you're married!'

Elisabeth made for the door. Mrs Marriott

attempted to catch hold of her arm, but in vain. Elisabeth walked rapidly into the hall with some wild idea of running out of the house even as she was, in light slippers and without a cloak. But before she reached the front door, it opened, and a grinning footman showed Sir Maurice in.

'My dear Elisabeth, is this wise? You should not run anywhere, at the moment.' He took her arm, and smilingly led her into the morning room.

At the first sight of him, her temper had cooled. His smile was the smile of a man who enjoys inflicting pain. She remembered someone telling her that he always smiled when about to kill his victims in a duel.

'I think we must send for the doctor again, Elisabeth.'

'No. I am quite well.'

'Mrs Marriott...' Elisabeth's aunt had followed her down, and was now hovering in the doorway. '...my dear Mrs Marriott, will you send a man for the doctor?'

'Aunt, do not leave me alone with this man. Sir Maurice, I must tell you that I cannot marry you tomorrow, or any other day!'

Sir Maurice continued to smile. The announcement did not seem to disturb him. Perhaps he had expected it. He said, over his shoulder to Mrs Marriott, 'Certainly your niece must be doctored. Her blood is too rich, and she is fevered. This has disarranged

183

her mind a trifle, and she must be purged, and bled. We must have her in trim for the ceremony tomorrow, must we not? Mrs Marriott, I think you may safely leave her in my hands while you send for the doctor.'

'Aunt!'

'My dear, I am sure Sir Maurice knows best. You are a wilful creature, and have never been checked before.'

'I know how to cure her of her wilfulness,' said Sir Maurice. 'Mrs Marriott, we are waiting for the doctor...'

With an apologetic look at Elisabeth, Mrs Marriott left the room.

ELEVEN

'I am sorry to have caused so much trouble,' said Elisabeth, keeping her voice steady with an effort, 'But I've changed my mind about marrying you, Sir Maurice.'

'Did you really think I'd let you escape me at the last minute?'

'You cannot force me to wed you.'

'Can I not? We are quite alone, as you see...'

'The servants...'

'Poof! They will not interfere, and neither will your aunt. I can do whatever I like with you, and nothing will be said. The doctor agrees with me that marriage will soon cure your girlish fancies. Be reasonable, my dear. Accept your fate with a smile. Who is there to come between us now?'

She was silent, but perhaps he knew the name that was in her mind.

He said, 'Did you think that base-born farmer could help you? Why, he can't even help himself, being in custody.'

'He was here today, in this very room, and I didn't notice any irons on his wrists.'

'So I heard.' Sir Maurice bared his teeth in his mirthless smile.

185

Elisabeth said, 'I suppose my footman informed you of his arrival...?'

'Yes, he sent a note by one of your grooms. What did the Squire want?'

Was there a trace of anxiety in Sir Maurice's voice?

'The Squire wanted to check on some papers that were in the secretaire here... Denys family papers ... some receipts for the painting of the miniatures, I think ... he seemed to treat Robin with courtesy.'

'No doubt. But your Robin went away again with the Squire, as soon as the latter was satisfied with the evidence?'

'Yes, I...'

She stopped, staring at the side of the fireplace. Where the miniatures of Robin's father and grandfather should have hung, there were two discoloured marks on the paper.

'What the deuce!' Sir Maurice leaped to his feet, and was across the room in a flash. Lips drawn back from his teeth, he revealed the face of a wolf for one horrible moment. And then his face smoothed out. He stood upright, and smiled.

'It seems the fellow is so obsessed with the miniatures that he has only to see them to steal them. They are indeed the instruments of his damnation!'

Elisabeth faltered out that perhaps the Squire might have taken them.

'What, without asking your permission? Surely not!'

Sir Maurice seated himself at the secretaire, took up a quill, and dipped it into the ink. 'The man could not have had a chance to dispose of them since leaving here, so they'll no doubt be found on him when a search is made. I'll write a note to the Squire at once, informing him of this fresh outrage.'

Elisabeth hid her face in her hands. Oh, Robin! How could you!

Sir Maurice rang the bell, and ordered the footman to send the note over to the Squire's place at once.

Elisabeth said, 'You treat my servants as if they were your own!'

'It was money well spent, to buy myself into their good graces, was it not? And in any case, they will soon be my servants in name as well as fact. Which reminds me that I've had my valet put my luggage in the bedroom opposite yours.'

'What, have you brought your things up here to the Hall? You intend to stay here tonight? How dare you?'

'Why not? We are properly chaperoned, are we not?'

'You know that we are not, since you yourself have corrupted my aunt!'

'You are talking wildly again, Elisabeth. In a little while the doctor will be here, and he'll give you a sleeping potion. No doubt you are overwrought, thinking of the morrow. No stranger shall approach you again while I am here.'

'I am not a child to be dosed and put to bed like that. And I am not ill.' She began to pace the room, biting her lip. She had feared Sir Maurice would find some way of coercing her. How could she escape him, if he took such precautions to keep her close?

'You see, Elisabeth, I have a confession to make. I started in pursuit of you with my eyes fixed more on your money than on your person...'

'If it is money you want from me, then I'll gladly loan you sufficient to cover your debts.'

'Strangely enough, your money has become of secondary importance. I would not let you go now, Elisabeth, though the devil himself demanded it.'

'It seems to me, sometimes, that you are the devil.'

He lifted his shoulders and let them fall. 'Very well. I am the devil, but I am also the man in possession, and I will not let you go to any man alive. If you did by chance escape me, I would follow wherever you went ... and make an end of you rather than let any other man have you.'

She put both hands to her throat.

'You understand me, don't you?' said Sir

188

Maurice. 'If you so much as smile on another man – on Robin Prior, or any other – then I will kill him as I'd kill a dog. I'm not making an idle boast. You realise that, don't you?'

She managed to nod, but could not speak.

'Well, then,' he said, 'Let us sit down and converse in amicable fashion, like any other civilised couple about to be married. You can see that there is no point in your having hysterics or throwing a tantrum. If, when the doctor arrives, you can tell me that you have decided to behave yourself, then I shall not insist on your being physicked now…'

She lifted her head in momentary hope.

'…but will save his skill for this evening. We shall keep closer than Darby and Joan today, my dear, and tonight the doctor shall give you a sleeping draught. Your maid shall sleep in your chamber with you, the footman outside your door … and I shall be across the corridor. In the morning you shall dress yourself as becomes a great lady … and then we will be wed and live happily ever after.'

He lifted her cold hand from her lap, put it to his lips, and waited for her to speak. She neither lifted her head, nor responded in any other way. He seemed satisfied that she was beaten.

'Am I your prisoner, then?' she said.

He made her a low bow. 'A prisoner of love.'

She set herself to play the part of down-trodden prisoner, and thought she succeeded tolerably well. Indeed, it was not hard to appear defeated, for Robin's latest escapade had hit her hard. How could he!

She allowed a few tears to fall, and because Sir Maurice looked pleased to see her tears this time, she did not try to check her grief. Let him think her broken in spirit, and he might be less careful in his watch on her.

All that day he stayed close by her side, and at night she was forced to drink a powerful sleeping draught before retiring to bed. Her maid slept in the same room. Her aunt lay next door, the footman across her door, and Sir Maurice across the corridor.

How was she to escape? She slept badly despite the potion, waking now and then to form plans … only to reject them a moment later.

When the barber arrived from Warwick next morning in order to dress her hair, she was beginning to feel desperate.

Since she had come into the country, Elisabeth had worn her hair dressed in loose curls and had refused to wear powder. But on the occasion of her marriage she was to appear once more as a lady of fashion. The barber would grease and powder her hair, and the whole process might take anything up to two hours.

While the barber laid out his tools, Elisabeth looked about her wildly for some way of escape ... but there was none. She was already dressed in chemise, corset, narrow petticoat and silk stockings. Now her maid brought up the unwieldy panniered framework which would hold out her skirts. This she tied on with tapes, firmly, about her mistress' waist.

Elisabeth could only just touch the outer edges of the panniers with her finger-tips. It was a very large framework because her best dress was extremely imposing, with huge wide skirts, and a train. Once inside all that material, she would have difficulty in walking fast, never mind running away.

The maid was bringing up her petticoats now, throwing them over Elisabeth's head, and tying them on with tapes at the back. Each petticoat was finished with deep ruffles, and the top one was also wired, to help hold out the weight of the skirts.

On the bed lay the cream and pink brocade dress in all its splendour. There was an underskirt of pink brocade, embroidered with gold. Over this would go a cream skirt, very full at sides and back, tied up with ribbons of blue. Then would come the cream bodice, with its elbow-length sleeves edged with falls of lace, and last of all the long cream brocade train would be fixed to

Elisabeth's shoulders.

The barber was poised, ready to begin. Elisabeth sank onto a low chair, and signed the maid to bring her a powdering gown, which would protect her and her clothes from the ubiquitous powder. She sat staring fixedly ahead while the barber got down to work.

The maid brought up Elisabeth's jewel case. 'What jewels will you wear today, my lady?'

'The pearls, I suppose.'

Suddenly she started. The barber protested, but she did not hear him, for she had been struck with an idea.

The two rings which she always wore, were missing. In the parlour yesterday morning, she had taken them off to give to Robin, he had refused to take them, and then she supposed she must have let them fall ... where? On the side-table? On the secretaire?

Usually she took off her rings herself, and set them on a table beside her bed last thing at night. They were not particularly valuable rings, but she had worn them since she was a young girl, and they meant a lot to her.

How could she turn their absence to advantage?

Sir Maurice came into the room, without knocking. Elisabeth flushed at his intrusion. He was dressed, save for waistcoat and coat. He bent over her hand.

'Are you quite well this morning, my dear?'

'Quite well, but worried about my rings. I must have dropped them in the parlour yesterday. I will go look for them presently.'

'I will send the footman to look for them.' He went to the door, and despatched the footman on the errand.

She shrugged, careful not to show that she was disappointed. If the footman found the rings, then she would have no excuse to leave the room.

He was looking at her jewel-case. 'You have many jewels, my dear. Are you sure that the rings you speak of are not here?'

Did he suspect something?

She spoke coldly. 'My maid will tell you that they are not there.'

'You are careless, my dear. It was only natural that I should check.'

She said icily, 'I have many jewels, but none that I value so highly. One was given me by my father, and the other by Sir William. I do not stir from this place without them.'

The footman came back. Luck was on her side, for he had found the little ring her father had given her, but not the other. The barber was building up the final row of curls.

Sir Maurice said, 'I will send the man to look again.'

'I daresay I will have to look myself. That man has proved a bad servant to me, and I swear he did not look properly.'

Sir Maurice shrugged. 'As you wish, my dear. I will accompany you downstairs myself when you are fully dressed... Barber, come to me as soon as you have finished my lady's head. I am not pleased with the set of my side curls.'

He kissed his hand to Elisabeth, and left. She pushed the one ring onto her finger, and tried not to fidget.

At length the final curl was in place, and the barber packed away his things in order to attend Sir Maurice.

'Shall I paint your face before you put on your dress, my lady?' said the maid, laying out the pots.

Elisabeth stood, with a yawn. 'First I'll see what has happened to that rogue of a footman and my ring. Do you think he could have pocketed it for himself?'

'Oh, no; my lady. He wouldn't dare!'

'I'm not so sure of that. If he's already sold me to Sir Maurice, then why shouldn't he rob me, too? Or you, for that matter.'

'Oh, my lady. You shouldn't say such things. I'm sure I've always served you faithfully...'

'Then help me find my ring. Or help me to get it back from that rogue of a footman, if he has pocketed it.'

'But Sir Maurice said...' The maid looked longingly at the door of Sir Maurice's room, as they went out into the corridor.

'I know he has given you money,' said Elisabeth, making for the stairs, 'But surely he would approve of your helping me to find my ring!'

'Yes, my lady, but...'

They were at the foot of the stairs. So far so good. In the hall there was a gardener and his boy arranging a stand of flowers, two maids polishing furniture, and Sir Maurice's groom leaning against the front door. Doubtless he had been stationed there to see that no-one left the house.

He addressed not Elisabeth, but her maid. 'Where be the lady going?'

'To my own parlour, fool!' said Elisabeth. 'If no-one else can find my ring, then I suppose I must look for it myself!'

She swept on into the parlour. As she had suspected, the footman was not looking for the ring very hard. In fact, he was lounging at his ease in a chair before the fire.

He came to his feet, looking sheepish.

'You see how well I am served,' said Elisabeth to her maid. 'Go tell Sir Maurice how the man flouts me...' She stamped her foot. 'I will have him dismissed at once, I swear it!'

'My lady!' protested the footman. 'I have looked everywhere...'

Elisabeth's maid joined in the condemnation. 'You weren't looking very hard just now, I must say. I'll tell Sir Maurice of your conduct this instant. Doubtless, as my lady says, you've pocketed the ring yourself!'

She ran out, leaving the footman to back away, blustering.

'My lady, I swear...'

'Down on your knees, fellow! Search the cracks in the floorboards over by the secretaire.'

The footman, cowed, got down on his hands and knees, and began to look for the missing jewel in earnest.

On the side table were arranged some pieces of plate, and a heavy vase. Elisabeth picked up the vase and brought it down on the back of the footman's head. He fell forward, and lay still.

The windows were high and narrow. Could she possibly get through one of them and be out of the park before the alarm was raised?

The door opened, and Elisabeth turned in a panic. Behind her the footman lay as one dead.

It was the housekeeper. For one moment Elisabeth felt faint, but then she noticed that the woman was holding her fingers to her lips, indicating that Elisabeth should keep silence.

'Hasn't he found it yet, my lady?' said the

housekeeper, in a carrying voice. She was looking down at the footman as she spoke, so she must have realised what had happened.

'Not yet, the rogue,' said Elisabeth. 'Oh, when Sir Maurice hears of this!'

The housekeeper shut the door firmly. She said, in a rapid voice, 'My lady, believe me, I had no idea that all was not well until yesterday. Squire Hartley warned me ... he asked me to be on the look-out ... and then I made discreet enquiries among those servants whom I thought I could trust, and learned that many of the household were in Sir Maurice's pay. The Squire said to remind you that Mr Prior will be waiting for you at the inn today.'

'But how to escape? I cannot get through the window, dressed like this.'

Elisabeth tore off her voluminous powdering gown, and attacked the tapes which tied on her layers of petticoats. The housekeeper got out her scissors, and snipped away till at last the petticoats and the panniered framework crumpled to the floor, and Elisabeth stepped out, clad only in chemise, corset and narrow petticoat. Her shoes were of satin with high red heels, and totally unsuitable for walking, but they would have to do. She bundled the powdering gown back about her, pulled up a stool, mounted it, and scrambled through the narrow window.

'Make haste, my lady,' said the house-keeper, as she thrust the discarded clothing behind the secretaire. 'I'll hold them off as long as I can... I fear you must walk, for there is one of Sir Maurice's men in the stables...'

Elisabeth lifted her skirts and ran across the formal garden into the shrubbery beyond. Once there, she paused to look back. The housekeeper was closing the parlour window. Smoke rose from various chimneys. Everything looked peaceful.

She turned away from the house and plunged down the nearest walk. This would skirt the paddock, and lead her directly into the park behind. To cross the park in a straight line would be to expose herself to view ... and if Sir Maurice were to discover her escape and order horses up from the stables ... or dogs...

She ran and ran, till her heart thumped, and she could barely see. Her gown billowed out as she ran, and caught on branches.

She realised that she could be seen easily from a distance, because she was wearing a light-coloured gown. She wished she could discard it, but she was not wearing enough beneath. Her petticoat also hampered her, being narrow, with many ruffles.

She paused, her hand to her side. She had already come a considerable distance ... and the village was in sight ... and there was yet no sound of pursuit.

Should she risk running across this last piece of rough ground in a straight line ... without so much as a single tree to offer cover?

She could see the lane that led into the lower end of the village ... if she could reach that ... no matter how fast Sir Maurice were to ride her down, she could scream and people in the village would hear her, and come to her rescue.

But what if he were to ride her down before she reached the village?

Then she heard it, the cry of the hunting-horn ... the long, echoing call, and the barking of dogs. Both came from the Hall.

With a gasp of fear she gathered herself together, and swift as any hunted fox, she ran for the village and safety. She thought she heard the thunder of galloping hooves ... and sobbed aloud as she fell upon the gate that led to the lane. The gate was stiff, and heavy. She must climb it, or cower there till she was captured.

She hurt her hands, climbing over the gate, and lost the remains of one shoe, and then at last she was slipping and stumbling along the lane, and passing between two cottages. She had thought to appeal for help to the first villager she saw, but all the cottages seemed empty. She could not understand it.

Then she realised that as this was supposed to be her wedding day, everyone would be on the village green, watching as the ox was roasted over an open fire.

She glanced down at herself. She was much splashed and grimed with mud, and her powdering gown was rent from hip to hem. Her one remaining shoe was split, and her carefully piled-up hair was coming down about her ears. She must look like a mad beggar-woman.

But she must reach Robin and get into the chaise which he had promised to have waiting, and then perhaps at Warwick they could stop for a few minutes to buy some clothes for her.

She could not face the stares of the villagers, but made her way round to the back of the inn, to ask a passing servant girl for Mr Prior.

'For who?' The girl stared at Elisabeth in amazement.

'There is a gentleman staying here ... possibly with some friends ... he was expecting me this morning.'

'Oh, those gentlemen!' The girl told Elisabeth to wait in the yard. Obviously she did not look respectable enough to be allowed inside the inn.

Elisabeth sank onto a bench, and tried to do something with her hair. She disentangled the two ropes of pearls which the barber had set on top of her coiffure. There was a pump nearby, at which she washed her hands and face. Then she pulled the pins out of her hair, shook it out and tied it back with a ribbon from her petticoat.

'Elisabeth?' It was Robin, looking shaken. 'What on earth has happened?' He picked her up, and held her to him. She clung to him, immeasurably thankful to be safe for the moment. She felt tears come, and let them fall.

'Your feet!' Robin exclaimed. 'My darling, what has happened?' He took off his velvet coat, and wrapped it around her.

In reaction, she found she was stammering. 'I – I'm all r – right, now … but Sir Maurice! Oh, Robin! He t – tried to keep me prisoner … set my own servants against me… I had to climb out of the window and I ran all the way here and I think he set the dogs on me!'

'What? The scoundrel! You are trembling!' His chin came out, and his eyes blazed. 'I hope he does follow you here, Elisabeth, for if he does, then…!'

She was alarmed at his anger. 'No, Robin! It was nothing! I am perfectly all right now, and quite ready to set off at once. You do have the chaise ready, don't you?'

Robin started. 'I have something better than a chaise for you!'

He carried her through a dark passageway

into the private room of the inn. This was a comfortable, dark panelled room, overlooking the green. There was a cheerful fire in it.

Around a table sat three gentlemen, who sprang to their feet with exclamations of dismay when they saw Elisabeth in her bedraggled state.

'She's all right!' said Robin. 'But she's had a bad fright. That devil sat a guard on her, but she slipped out of the window and ran here.'

'The blackguard!' swore a neatly-dressed man in black.

'Mr Deeds!' cried Elisabeth. 'Oh, how glad I am to see you!'

'I told you she'd have a hard time getting away!' A big, red-faced man shook his fist in the approximate direction of the Hall and Sir Maurice.

'Squire Hartley!' Elisabeth shrank into Robin's shoulder.

'It's all right,' said Robin, depositing her in a chair, and giving her a reassuring smile. 'They're all on your side.'

The remaining member of the party was a stranger to her.

'Oh,' said Mr Deeds, 'This is a colleague of mine… I thought that if you took to him, he might act as steward for you. We were all coming over to the Hall to prevent the marriage. You didn't think we'd let him marry you out of hand, did you? Why, what would old Sir William have said, if I'd been so remiss in my duties...'

'Or I, his neighbour,' said the Squire.

'Or I,' said Robin. He seated himself beside Elisabeth and poured out some wine for her.

Elisabeth took one gulp, refused more, and put her hand on Robin's shoulder. 'Robin, have you the chaise ready? You know we must be off...'

'No need of that,' said Robin.

'Oh, but there is, indeed!' cried Elisabeth. 'How can I make you understand!'

'It is you who don't understand,' said Robin. 'Did you really think I was in danger of going to prison for stealing those miniatures?'

Elisabeth turned to the Squire. 'Now that's another thing. Squire, I must tell you that I don't wish to prosecute Robin for taking those miniatures, despite everything Sir Maurice says.'

'Well, you couldn't, could you?' said the Squire, with a slight smile. He didn't seem perturbed, and neither did the others.

'You see, my darling,' said Robin. 'I showed the Squire the Will, and then the receipts which Sir William had stored in the secretaire ... receipts for the painting of the miniatures ... and then I showed him the inventory which had been made of the contents of the Hall, and he saw for himself that the entries describing those two particular miniatures had been crossed out and initialled not by me, but by Mr Deeds...'

'You mean that it wasn't you who altered the inventory? I was so sure that it was!'

'Why would I do a thing like that? The miniatures are mine.'

'Oh, Robin! I wish you wouldn't persist in that lie...'

'You see, gentlemen?' Robin turned to the others, who burst out laughing. 'Elisabeth, my dearest; Sir William left me the two miniatures in his Will. I am afraid that you never read it right through, did you?'

'Well, no. Mr Deeds had already told me the parts which affected me. You mean that you really are the legal owner of the miniatures?'

'I'm more than that,' said Robin, blushing. 'I'm afraid you're in for a shock, Elisabeth. You see, I'm your landlord. Sir William left me Denys Hall in his Will. Or rather, the property was entailed on me.'

Elisabeth gaped.

Mr Deeds said, 'Aren't you forgetting something, Sir Robert?'

'"Sir Robert?"' repeated Elisabeth, in a faint voice.

'Oh, that!' said Robin, going fiery red and fidgeting with his cravat. 'Well, I don't suppose I shall ever get round to using the title!'

TWELVE

Mr Deeds explained.

'I've served the Denys family man and boy, and so did my father before me, so I suppose I know most if not all of the family secrets. Sir William never married, as you know. Some say he wanted the lady his brother won to wife, and it's certain that he was very shaken when she died soon after her husband. Sir William took the boy – that was your father, Sir Robert – and brought him up as his own.

'Perhaps he loved the boy too much, I can't tell. One moment the lad was over-indulged, and the next he was whipped for a trifling fault. Sir William wished his nephew to make a good marriage, and had an heiress looked out for him. The girl was well enough, but the boy turned sullen and would not pay his addresses to her. Sir William raged in vain, and the heiress departed to wed another.

'That year the lad took to hunting every day the hounds were out. Sometimes he'd stay a week or so with friends, so that he could ride with a pack which hunted on the far side of Warwick. I don't think he encountered Miss Prior on the hunting field...'

'No, indeed,' said Robin. 'My mother disapproved of money spent on such pastimes. They met at an Assembly in Warwick, and he stood up with her for one of the country dances.'

'Miss Prior was a lady of extraordinary strength of character,' said Mr Deeds, 'As well as great beauty. I must say that she made a great and lasting impression on me. I do not wonder that your father was struck dumb at the sight of her, nor that he followed her home and refused to leave the neighbourhood till she had accepted him.'

Robin continued the tale. 'Naturally, Sir William was furious, but so also was my grandfather Prior, who in his own words "Didn't hold with the nobility". He locked my mother up in the attic and refused to let her out till she promised to give up seeing my father...'

'...who took the time-honoured way out of the dilemma by way of a ladder and a pair of horses spurring through the night to Warwick...'

'...with both families hot in pursuit...'

'How romantic!' said Elisabeth, wide-eyed.

Robin looked down his nose. 'It ought to have been handled better. Both sides of the family were furious, and there was a scandal...'

'But didn't they marry?' Elisabeth asked

Mr Deeds.

'Bless me, yes! Of course! I was present at the wedding, which took place from the house of a friend of the Prior family in Warwick, and after a few days I managed to persuade old man Prior to receive his daughter again.

'But Sir William was a different kettle of fish. He refused to see the newly-weds, and he gave orders that they should never be admitted again. He declared that he did not believe that they were married, that Miss Prior had trapped his nephew into making a false declaration of passion ... well, he said a great many things which it would have been wiser not to have said. He told me he'd forgive his nephew and re-instate him as his heir when the latter gave up his "light of love", as he called Miss Prior, and admitted the error of his ways.'

Robin laughed. 'As if my father would!'

Elisabeth said, 'And did they live happily ever after?'

'Yes, and no,' said Robin with a sigh. 'They fought a lot, they tell me, but I can only remember them walking into a room with their arms about each other, and my grandfather told me he never saw a man dote on a woman as my father did. Perhaps my father might have settled down to the life of a gentleman farmer in the end, though I think it somewhat unlikely...'

'So do I,' said Mr Deeds, with an unexpected grin. 'He had expensive tastes, as I recall.'

'And my grandfather Prior had to foot the bill,' said Robin. 'But my father only lived three years after the marriage, and then he caught a fever and faded away. My mother could have married again, of course, but she never seemed to be interested in other men. I was brought up strictly, sent to the best schools, and then on to University ... but it was dinned into my head both by my mother and my grandfather that the nobility were an idle, spendthrift, wasteful lot, giving to gaming, and heavy drinking and grinding the faces of the poor. Naturally I heard no good of Sir William Denys, and when he tried to make me his heir...'

Elisabeth gave a little start. 'That was the year I first met you?'

'Yes. He had other relations, descendants of cousins and the like. That year he decided to have us all to stay at the Hall, to look us over. He seemed to like me, and after I won that race, he informed me that as the estates were entailed on me anyway, he wished me to stay on at the Hall and learn how to be a gentleman. I was under no circumstances to communicate with my mother and grandfather again. Naturally, I refused.'

'Oh!' cried Elisabeth. 'Did Sir William disinherit you, only to leave all his money to me? I wish I'd known!'

'What could you have done about it?' said Robin, laughing. 'I was doing well enough on the Home Farm, and I wanted nothing more out of life than to jog along in the same old way. If I thought of Sir William at all, it was with anger, that he should have been so contemptuous of the Prior family. I was proud of being a Prior, and I wanted nothing to do with Denys Hall. And then one day I had a letter from Mr Deeds advising of Sir William's death. Shortly after, Mr Deeds came to see me, with a copy of the Will. He asked for instructions, and I told him to go to the Devil!'

'No, you were not pleased to see me,' said Mr Deeds, with a reminiscent smile. 'You see, Lady Elisabeth, Sir Robert had been brought up to despise great landowners and the bearers of ancient titles, and Sir William's death had brought him both. He wanted nothing to do with his inheritance. He made the point – a valid one – that as he couldn't afford to live there, he might as well ignore it. Now I knew that you wanted to rent the place, and it was the work of a moment to get Sir Robert's agreement to that.'

'I thought I was well rid of the place,' said Robin, 'And then everything began to tangle itself into the most confounded mess. For some reason best known to himself, Sir

William had stipulated that I visit the Hall and remove the two miniatures of my father and grandfather in person. I did want the miniatures ... so when Mr Deeds wrote to me saying that I must take them on such and such a day in the following week because you were going to move in ... well, it was damned inconvenient. I rode over to the Hall to meet Mr Deeds and his clerk...'

'That was the day you were supposed to take possession, my lady,' said Mr Deeds. 'I wanted him to stay, to meet you, but he declined. He took the miniatures, had a glass of wine with me in the hall, and left...'

'I was in a shocking temper,' said Robin. 'I hadn't liked seeing the state that the Hall was in ... and the village ... and then there were no servants waiting to greet you ... everything in disarray. I was angry ... with you ... with myself ... for what seemed like running away ... ducking my responsibilities to my tenants...'

'I tried to interest him in you, my lady,' said Mr Deeds, 'But he would not listen ... and then he passed you on the road just when you needed help...'

'...and you did not recognise me,' said Robin, putting his arm about Elisabeth. 'And I did not wish to embarrass you by telling you my real name and title. I found I simply could not say that I was Sir Robert Denys of Denys Hall. And so, thinking I would assist you to safety and then leave you … I said only that my name was Robin Prior.'

Elisabeth said. 'But when we got to the Hall, there was so much to be done, and you took pity on me…?'

Robin glanced at Mr Deeds, with a smile '…yes, even though Mr Deeds thought it most unseemly for me to wait on you. I had to be very firm with him, because he wanted to tell you the truth…'

Elisabeth laughed. 'Perhaps I would have boxed your ears, if I'd known!'

'Perhaps.' His smile vanished. 'But by that time I knew I couldn't leave you. I had to stay. You offered me a way of doing so, as your steward … and this meant I could also help my poor tenants. Naturally I leapt at the chance.'

'How romantic!' murmured Elisabeth, with a naughty smile. 'And you always said you hadn't an ounce of romance in you!'

Robin tugged at his cravat. 'Well, it seems I could not help myself.'

Squire Hartley beamed at them both. 'He kept out of my way, the young dog. I would have given him away, if I'd caught a clear sight of him. I rode in the race round the Park myself, you know. Of course, I was a lot younger, then.'

'Yes,' said Robin. 'I had to keep out of the way of visitors. Although I hadn't been in the neighbourhood for some twelve years, the Squire here knew me the moment I walked into his study...'

'With the beadle on his heels...'

'...yes, with the Law on my tail. The Squire and I had a good laugh about that, and then set our heads together to see how we could outwit Sir Maurice. You see, the Squire's sons had been playing deep with our smiling gentleman and the Squire had been wondering how best to stop that caper. The lads are both under age, and therefore technically can't be held responsible for their debts.'

The Squire took up the story. 'I felt we should give Sir Maurice enough rope to hang himself with. Robin suggested we make enquiries in the neighbourhood and in London, about Sir Maurice. We drove into Warwick that very day to set out enquiries on foot, and then we went on to the Home Farm. Robin showed me his copy of the Will, which proved he was entitled to remove two miniatures from the Hall ... and later on, Lady Elisabeth, you were so kind as to let me check that the miniatures in question were the ones Robin had taken.'

'I took Robin back to my house to lodge for a while, but he was always wanting to be near the Hall, fearing I don't know what from yon fine gentleman...'

'With reason!' said Elisabeth, shuddering.

'You need fear him no longer,' said Mr Deeds. 'You will remember that Robin – that Sir Robert – wrote to me from the Hall some time ago, requesting I find you another steward...' And here he waved a hand towards that sober-suited gentleman, who had retired to sit in the background while all this was going on. '...which I accordingly did for you. At the same time Sir Robert asked if I knew anything about Sir Maurice Winton, who seemed to have designs on your lady-ship's fortune, and I set enquiries on foot in London about the gentleman.

'It seems Sir Robert's instinct was sound, for Sir Maurice has many debts, going back some years. There is also talk of a forged bond. In fact, there are a good many gentlemen in London who would be glad to lay their hands on Sir Maurice Winton, for a quiet chat.'

Elisabeth shrank further into the circle of Robin's arms. 'I must tell you that he threatened me yesterday ... and had a watch put on me. I found my servants refused to obey my orders, when I wanted to leave the house. I didn't know who to trust. Last night he drugged me with a sleeping draught, but today with the aid of the housekeeper I managed to slip out of the parlour window, and ran here...'

Fear took hold of her, remembering Sir Maurice's threats, and she grabbed one of

Robin's hands. 'Come, let us away … you promised me…!'

'There's no need for that,' said Robin, in soothing tones.

'You don't understand! He is a wicked man!'

'I can deal with him,' said Robin.

The innkeeper knocked and entered.

'Sirs, if you please, but here's Sir Maurice Winton come from the Hall, with dogs, following the trail of a maid who has stolen off with some of her mistress' clothing and jewels…'

'The devil!' said Robin.

'But,' said the innkeeper, squaring massive shoulders, 'If you'll pardon the liberty, I'm not happy about this. Miss here is no maid-servant, and though I've only seen her lady-ship twice, on horseback, it seems to me that this is her ladyship indeed. What's more, we've heard rumours here in the village that all is not well up at the Hall, and that her ladyship hasn't been free to come and go as she pleased. So if it's all the same to you, I'll get half a dozen stout lads together, and send the fine gentleman packing.'

'Thank you,' said Elisabeth, with tears in her eyes. 'It is good to know who are my friends.'

'Yes, indeed,' said Robin. 'Landlord, you need have no fear for the lady, since every-one in this room has her interests at heart.

Will you ask the gentleman to join us?'

The door was flung open, and in stalked Sir Maurice in a cold fury. He grasped Elisabeth's arm, apparently seeing no-one else in the room.

'So, you thought to escape me, did you? I'd have been here half an hour since but the damned groom mis-directed the dogs onto the trail of a kitchenmaid ... and if he did it on purpose, he'll not hold his post long!'

'That's enough!' said Robin. 'Unhand the lady, sirrah!'

Sir Maurice whirled about, and his jaw dropped. 'You! And the Squire?'

'This is Mr Deeds, the Lady Elisabeth's man of business, and this other gentleman here is her new steward.'

Sir Maurice took a step back, but recovered. 'Squire, why is that imposter not locked up in jail?'

'Why, Sir Maurice,' said the Squire, 'Perhaps because he is not an imposter, and has committed no particular crime that I know of. Allow me to introduce you to Sir Robert Denys, the owner of Denys Hall, and also of the miniatures which you thought he had stolen.'

Sir Maurice's face assumed the bony look of a skull. A red gleam came into his eyes.

'If that is so,' said Sir Maurice, giving every word its weight, 'Then I must tell you that I find your behaviour unpardonable ...

and most ungentlemanly. You have deceived me, and you have deceived the Lady Elisabeth. It seems my first impression of you was correct, and that you are nothing but a clod-hopping peasant at heart!'

Elisabeth rose to her feet with a cry. She knew such words as these were meant to provoke a duel ... and she knew how many men had been killed by Sir Maurice in duels.

Robin remained calm, but his chin came out, and his hand strayed to his side, where hung a pretty dress-sword.

He said, 'I knew from the moment I first set eyes on you, Sir Maurice, that it would come to this. Name your seconds, and I'll meet you wherever and whenever you wish.'

'No!' cried Elisabeth, and flung herself on Robin, only to be set aside.

'How delightfully stupid this young man is,' said Sir Maurice, exposing his teeth in his famous smile. 'I shall have much pleasure in despatching him into the next world at the earliest possible opportunity.'

'I doubt that,' said Robin, 'And if we can arrange...'

'I forbid it!' said Elisabeth. 'Robin, I wish to marry you, and not to bury you. Sir Maurice, you are in no position to challenge anyone to a duel, since there are warrants out for your arrest at this very moment, for debt and for forgery. If you linger in this neighbourhood to fight a duel, I shall see to it that you are arrested and suffer the fate you intended for Robin. You have half an hour to retrieve your belongings from the Hall and go, or it is I who will set the dogs on you!'

'Now wait a minute!' said Robin. 'I want to fight him, as much as he…'

'Well said!' shouted the Squire. 'I'm not in favour of duelling, either. Neither Mr Deeds here nor I will agree to act as seconds in a duel, and if you two gentlemen attempt to fight without seconds, then you'll be breaking the law, and as a magistrate I shall clap you both up in jail. And let me remind you, Sir Maurice, that once in jail you'll find it difficult to avoid being served with the writs at present on their way to you.'

Sir Maurice's eyes narrowed, and he reminded Elisabeth more than ever of a Death's Head. He bowed, went to the door, and vanished. Robin made as if to go after him, but the Squire stopped him.

'Thank the Lord for that!' said Mr Deeds. 'That is indeed an evil man, and I'm glad to have seen the last of him!'

The Squire laid his hand on Robin's shoulder, and gave him a push in Elisabeth's direction. 'There, we all know you'd have fought him if you could … you young gamecocks are all alike … but it's better for the Lady Elisabeth's reputation that there's no fight, and no scandal.'

'I suppose so,' said Robin, but he sounded unconvinced.

'I wonder,' said Mr Deeds, 'whether Sir Maurice paid in cash or in promises for the revelry here in the village … for the celebrations which cannot now take place…'

Elisabeth began to smile. 'The chaplain must be waiting for me up at the Hall … and my aunt … and our visitors … and my faithless servants…'

'Your faithful housekeeper will identify the rotten apples, and they shall all be swept away,' said Robin. 'And as for the celebration, let it go ahead, and I will pay for it, if Sir Maurice has not yet done so. After all, we do have something to celebrate, don't we?'

Elisabeth was suddenly aware of the ridiculous figure she must present, in bedraggled clothes, with her hair awry.

She said, 'I refuse to be proposed to like this! Mr Deeds, if you and my new steward will accompany me back to the Hall, to set everything to rights, and explain to my guests what has happened … and you will of course stay with me, and not here at the inn … and you, Squire, will your ladies be very distressed that there is no wedding today?'

'My lady,' said the Squire, with heavy gallantry. 'I daresay we'll all dance at your wedding yet … and with a lighter heart, if you take your Robin here as your husband.'

'I'll not remove to the Hall,' said Robin, looking flustered. 'I fear it would not be thought correct...'

'You'll stay with me,' said the Squire, slapping him on the back.

'Yes,' said Robin. 'I'd like that, but first I must speak with Elisabeth in private ... we have various things to discuss...'

Elisabeth gave him her hand. 'Call on me this evening, at six. I daresay you may find me at home, perhaps walking in the ruins...'

Six hours later, the charmingly-dressed lady who wandered in the ruins of Denys Hall bore little resemblance to the scarecrow of that morning.

Elisabeth's hair had been dressed in loose flowing curls. There were panniers to hold out the stiffened blue skirts of her brocade dress, cut in the Shepherdess style, with gracefully swinging full skirts, and tiny ruffles of lace about the throat and at the edges of the low-cut bodice.

On her head perched a tiny straw hat ornament with blue ribbons, and more blue ribbons appeared in bows down the front of her dress.

Elisabeth was very aware of the pretty picture she presented to the world, and was only anxious that Robin should arrive soon to appreciate it.

She looked back at the house, where all lay

quiet beneath the late afternoon sun. Mr Deeds and the Squire were in the library, smoking their pipes and discussing business, while her new steward was making a tour of the house with the housekeeper. Mrs Marriott was weeping as one of the maids packed her belongings. Perhaps Elisabeth would relent and allow her aunt a small pension in due course, but the sooner she was out of the house, the better.

When would Robin come? She was in a fever to see him, waiting was intolerable.

Someone whistled, close by. She started, and looked around. She was in full view of the house here, but the whistle came from further in the ruins. She smiled. Of course, Robin would not wish to meet her in a spot from which everyone could see them!

She picked up her skirts and ran lightly back into the ruins. As she stepped through a low arch, so a heavy cloak was thrown over her head, and she was lifted from the ground by a pair of strong arms.

For a moment she was paralysed with shock, and then her senses began to inform her that this was not Robin playing a trick on her.

She struggled, kicking wildly. In vain. She was being carried over rough ground ... and now she could hear someone muttering instructions ... the footsteps left the turf, and were now on beaten earth.

She kicked again, and then someone caught both her ankles in a firm clasp ... something was being bound about them, so that she could no longer separate her feet ... and she was stifling in the folds of that heavy cloak...

She was going to faint ... she could barely stir a finger, she felt so weak ... she felt herself falling, and landed with a thump that shook all the remaining breath out of her.

She glimpsed daylight, and tried to take a deep breath of air, but the cloak descended more closely yet about her neck and shoulders. Something hard was being passed about her shoulders, and bound tight. She sobbed aloud and was set upright, in the corner of a chair...

Not a chair. She could move her hands a little way and they informed her that she was sitting on leather. Then she heard the horses' hooves, and knew that she was in a coach, being driven away from everything that life held dear.

The cloak was drawn off her head and shoulders, and she was not surprised to see Sir Maurice, seated opposite her, his teeth gleaming.

'Are you going to scream, or try to bite me?' he asked. 'I will gag you if you try it. I think I can say I'm prepared for any eventuality. We will soon be off Denys land and then ... where shall we go? Paris? Rome? I shall be happy to fall in with your wishes, my dear.'

She set her lips hard. She would not let him see that she was sick with fear.

'I'd planned to marry you first, and carry you abroad afterwards,' said Sir Maurice, 'but I fear you have made that impossible. We shall be married in due course ... in Rome or Naples, perhaps ... you'll be begging me to make an honest woman of you in a few days' time.'

She was trembling with fear, but trying not to show it.

'As for your gallant clod-hopper, Robin Prior, my wrist aches to make an end of him. Perhaps he'll be so foolhardy as to follow us abroad, and then I can dispose of him at my leisure. You'd like to watch that, wouldn't you?'

She closed her eyes, and turned her face away from him. They were travelling fast, too fast for comfort over rutted country lanes. She was thrown violently to one side as they rounded a bend and she regained her place in the corner with some difficulty. Sir Maurice bent forward and loosened the belt which had bound her arms to her body, leaving only one strap about her ankles. He indicated that she hang onto the tasselled thong that hung from the side of the carriage for such purposes.

She looked out through the window, only to see that they were coming to the end of the wood. In a moment they would take the hill down to the ford ... the ford where Robin had rescued her before...

Oh, Robin! Where are you now?

There was a cry from the coachman above.

'Sir Maurice! There's a man on horseback across the ford...!'

THIRTEEN

Sir Maurice threw down the window, and put out his head.

Elisabeth did the same at her side, but the swaying of the coach made it difficult for her to be sure who was sitting on the horse in the middle of the ford. Only, her heart told her that it must be Robin.

An ominous sound caused her to look around. Sir Maurice had taken one of a pair of pistols from the side pocket of his coach, and had cocked it ready to fire.

'Coward!' she said.

'This pistol is a defence against highwaymen, my dear ... not against lovers. If he takes the part of a highwayman, and tries to hold us up, then I'm entitled to shoot him dead!'

They were going even faster now... Sir Maurice was braced against the seat on which she sat, and she was hanging on to her thong for dear life ... they were swaying from side to side ... but the coachman could not enter the ford at that pace with safety, and was even now applying the brakes. Waves of water arose on either side of the coach, and for a moment Sir Maurice drew back from the open window, cursing as he was drenched with water.

Then the door at his side of the coach was wrenched open, and a brown hand reached inside to seize Sir Maurice's wrist ... the wrist that held the cocked pistol ... and Sir Maurice was drawn out of the coach with a cry, and pitched headlong into the river below.

Feverishly Elisabeth fought her way out of the bonds that held her ankles, and leaped onto the one remaining pistol, which was still in its holster. She remembered to cock it ... so.

Then she groped to the open door of the chaise and looked out.

Sir Maurice had fallen face down into the river, coming to rest on his hands and knees. His wig had come off in his fall, and his skull gleamed bald in the sunlight. He staggered to his feet, dripping wet.

Before Elisabeth could speak, Robin's strong arm lifted her bodily out of the coach, and she was transported back to the Denys side of the river. There a gently-sloping greensward lay between the water and the trees. As he made to put her down on the turf, she clung round Robin's neck.

'Let him go ... don't leave me!'

'You will be safe here. If anything should happen to me, then run back up into the wood. Mr Deeds and the Squire are on their way here with reinforcements, but since they did not know the paths through the woods, they may be some minutes yet!'

He kissed her hard and swift, and then dropped her onto the turf. Only then did she realise that she was still clutching the spare pistol from the coach. She would have offered it to Robin, but by that time he was already on his way back into the water.

Sir Maurice had rescued his dripping wig and clapped it back, anyhow on his head. He was still grinning but now more than ever, it was the grin of death. He was also still brandishing his pistol.

'You shall die for this, you impudent rogue!' swore Sir Maurice, aiming at Robin's head.

Robin laughed. Sir Maurice pulled the trigger and nothing happened.

'I fear,' said Robin, with elaborate courtesy, 'that the powder in your pistol must have become wet when you tumbled into the water.' His eyes flashed with sudden fury. 'Now fight fair, you blackguard!'

Sir Maurice began to wade back to the bank, but stopped when he came to his coach. He shook his fist at his valet and coachman, who were sitting on top of the vehicle. 'Why didn't you fire on him, fellows? Can't you see he's a highwayman? Bring the chaise back out of the ford and secure the lady within, while I make an end of this impudent rogue!'

'Not so fast!' Elisabeth levelled her pistol at the coachman. 'I have no desire to step back into that conveyance... Coachman, take yourself off to the far side of the river, if you please!'

'A good idea!' Robin brought his riding crop down on the haunch of the nearest carriage horse, and the chaise began slowly to cross the ford, to the opposite bank.

'I shall kill you slowly for this, my lad!' Sir Maurice began to inch himself out of his sodden velvet coat. 'I shall make you cry for mercy!'

Robin laughed, but his eyes still blazed with anger. He tethered his mare to the branch of a tree, and stripped off his own coat, too.

Elisabeth wanted to beg Robin not to fight, but one look at his hard young face told her it would do no good. He must run onto his destiny, just as young Henry Dart had done ... and so many others...

She resolved that if ... when ... Sir Maurice killed Robin, then she would fire the villain's own pistol into his very heart ... and then there would be an end of everything.

'On guard!' Sir Maurice was made of steel, it seemed. His recent ducking might never have happened, to judge by the speed and ferocity with which he sprang on Robin.

At that moment Robin had only half-drawn his sword from his scabbard and was forced to give ground, stumbling back as best he could.

Sir Maurice's sword-point flickered within an inch of Robin's cravat before the latter could get his own sword up. The blades clashed and slithered, revolving, twisting high to the left and low to the right...

There was a stamp of heels, and they disengaged.

'Saha!' said Sir Maurice, grinning. 'Does he think he knows how to fence, then? Has he had a few lessons? Pooh! A child, merely! Have at you!'

Robin was silent, watchful ... with his chin tucked in, and his brows drawn flat in a frown, he concentrated on Sir Maurice. His foot slid along the turf until the blades once again caught, and twisted.

Again Sir Maurice pressed his opponent hard, the lines deepening between nose and chin as he used his years of experience to overwhelm the young man ... and Robin gave more ground.

Sir Maurice laughed aloud. 'Why, this will soon be over, and I'd thought to provide some sport for the lady. Have at you again!'

Once more there was a swift rush of feet, and the swords glittered and swung. Robin gave ground yet again, allowing himself to be driven away from the trees and down towards the water.

'Please God, save him!' Elisabeth clasped the pistol with both hands.

Sir Maurice fought with his left arm outstretched behind him to act as a balance. Robin fought in different style, with his left arm bent, the hand resting on his hip. It was a less flamboyant style, but efficient.

They were nearing the water's edge. Robin stepped back into the water, and side-stepped out of it, only to turn swiftly on Sir Maurice, and drive him into the water instead.

'What the...!' Sir Maurice staggered, splashing as he went along the causeway. 'Why, you young...'

Robin leaped into the water after his adversary, and now it was hard to tell which of the men was gaining the mastery, and which losing it. They fought their way back along the causeway to the middle, and then with a sudden burst of power, Sir Maurice pressed Robin all the way back to the bank on which Elisabeth stood.

Still Robin did not speak.

Sir Maurice was no longer as fresh as he had been. Perhaps for the first time in many years he had come across an adversary worthy of his steel ... perhaps he now wished for some of the youth he had squandered in hours of debauchery.

They were back on the turf again. Elisabeth could discern a sheen of sweat on Robin's forehead and upper lip, though his arm seemed untiring, and his feet carried him without a stumble.

From Sir Maurice's open mouth came the puff of exertion. The man's face was grey and streaked with sweat.

'Back, Elisabeth!' It was the first time that Robin had spoken.

The two men were now so close to her that Sir Maurice could reach out and grasp her arm. She fell to her knees, trying to run out of his way. For a moment Robin's concentration was broken.

'I have you now!' cried Sir Maurice, and his blade sneaked up.

Robin leaped back, and the two men halted, facing one another, both breathing hard.

'This pays for all!' said Sir Maurice, lunging forward. And now he rushed on his opponent with such fury that it looked as if Robin's guard must be broken at last.

Robin proved equal to the moment. With a gliding movement he sidestepped Sir Maurice's rush, and at the same time he engaged his sword, and thrust Sir Maurice's blade upwards ... and then Sir Maurice went plunging on without his weapon to sprawl full length on the grass.

Robin collected Sir Maurice's sword, and tossed it far out into the river.

Sir Maurice lay where he had fallen. His wig had once more come adrift, his eyes burned with hate, and his teeth gleamed in the forced grin of the devil at bay.

'Up!' said Robin.

'Kill me quickly!' said Sir Maurice. He got to his knees, and held out his arms.

'No,' said Robin.

'But you must!' Sir Maurice got to his feet. His fingers curved into the claws of a predatory animal.

'Take care!' cried Elisabeth. 'He's going to spring on you!'

'I would not kill him, even then,' said Robin. 'He would like me to kill him, but I prefer that he should live, and suffer a living death. Sir Maurice, look about you at this pleasant scene. It will be the last sight of freedom you will have for many a year, if not for life.'

Among the trees, where the road ran down to the ford, men were waiting, some on horseback, some in a gig.

Two of the men now came down the slope to where Sir Maurice stood in his shirt-sleeves and sodden breeches.

'Sir Maurice Winton, I arrest you in the name of the King!' said a stout man in a red waistcoat. With a start, Elisabeth remembered that the unfashionable red waistcoat was always worn by Bow Street Runners.

'What is the charge?' said Sir Maurice in a

hoarse voice.

'Forgery, and extortion, practised on a feeble-minded but wealthy young man. I gather there are also warrants out for your arrest for debt, but this one of mine takes precedence, being a capital charge.'

Sir Maurice looked wildly around. 'You are mistaken. I am not the man you seek…'

'Come along quietly,' said the man in the red waistcoat, producing a pair of handcuffs from behind his back, and fastening them on his prisoner with professional ease. 'You've already been identified by Squire Hartley here, and I owe him and Mr Deeds a vote of thanks for putting me on your trail, for when you left London, no-one knew where you'd gone.'

Sir Maurice's face seemed to have fallen in, as if his teeth could no longer support his jawbone.

'May I make a suggestion?' said Robin. 'Sir Maurice's chaise is over there, piled high with his luggage. Why don't you travel back to London in that, instead of the gig? At least the chaise can be sold to defray his debts.'

'Talking of creditors,' said the Squire, who was searching the pockets of Sir Maurice's discarded velvet coat. 'I'm looking for some IOUs which my young lads were so foolish as to have given this man … ah, here they are! We'll have a bonfire with them tonight!'

The Bow Street Runner saluted Elisabeth, and the Squire. 'Then I'll bid you farewell, gents ... and lady!' He pushed Sir Maurice down towards the causeway, and his prisoner went without a word, stumbling along in a dream.

The Squire took the pistol out of Elisabeth's hand, and carefully made it safe. He said, 'Well, it seems the gig would be free to take the little lady back to the Hall, if she so wishes?'

Robin put his arm around Elisabeth. He said, 'History repeats itself. Will you go back in the gig, or will you ride with me?'

Elisabeth put her arms about his neck.

'I'll go with you, my love. Wherever and whenever you wish.'

The wedding of Sir Robert Denys to the Lady Elisabeth Silverwood was celebrated with much rejoicing a month later. Afterwards, the young couple paid a visit to the old tithe barn, where a feast had been laid out for their tenants, together with every man, woman and child from the village who could walk ... and some who had been brought there in carts.

Within the Hall itself there were more guests. There were flowers everywhere, and a great noise of fiddlers, playing madly away. It seemed that half the County had come to congratulate the young couple on their marriage.

In one corner the Squire was boasting to his cronies of the way in which he had contrived the capture of that notorious desperado, Sir Maurice Winton, now awaiting trial in a London jail. In another, the housekeeper was rushing up another batch of jellies and sweetmeats to a table which seemed to be cleared of food as fast as it was laid. The new steward, a quiet man, looked on benignly from the head of the stairs.

Even Mrs Marriott was there, somewhat subdued, but already beginning to boast that she had early on divined there was more to Robin Prior than he had let on! Elisabeth's anger towards her aunt had soon softened, and it seemed likely that Mrs Marriott would not be shut off from the new family circle at the Hall.

Later that day, the young married couple found themselves alone in the library with Mr Deeds, who had requested a few minutes of their time on a matter of some importance.

'I am going to let you into one last secret,' said Mr Deeds. He busied himself pouring out three glasses of a rare old port he had discovered in the cellars.

'This port was laid down by Sir William many years ago. He thought it might come in handy at a celebration, and so I say we should drink it now.'

'To Sir William,' said Robin, with his arm about his very new wife. Indeed, Robin's arm seemed rarely to stray from his wife's waist these days.

'What is this last secret?' said Elisabeth.

'Sir William came to regret that he had parted with young Robin on harsh terms, and many a time he said to me afterwards that he wished the lad would write to him ... or make the first move towards reconciliation in some way.'

'I wish I'd known,' said Robin.

'I doubt if you would have done anything about it,' said his fond wife.

'Perhaps not,' said her husband, smiling down at her. 'But if I'd had you at my side, perhaps I wouldn't have been so unforgiving. I feel a different person since I've known you, Elisabeth.'

'Harrum!' said Mr Deeds, as the young couple appeared to forget his existence for the time being. 'What I'd to tell you was that on his death-bed Sir William told me that he was not going to alter his Will, but that he wished, if possible, to bring you together ... the lad whose blood ran in his veins, and the girl whom he loved like a father.

'He reminded me that the two of you had once had a fondness for one another, and he wondered if that fondness might not be revived, if you could be brought together here, under this roof, once more. He was

236

dying and he knew it. He tried to make me swear I'd contrive a meeting between you, but of course that would have been unethical. However, when I suggested that he write in a codicil to his Will, stating that Robin must collect his two miniatures from the Hall in person, he agreed to do so.

'That, Sir Robin, was the reason I wanted to keep you here on the day that Lady Elisabeth was expected to take possession of this place. Naturally I was surprised when you offered to work for her, but on reflection I felt that Sir William might not have been displeased.

'If he is looking down on us now,' said Mr Deeds, raising his glass to the portrait over the fireplace, 'then I hope he thinks I have discharged his last commission satisfactorily.'

Robin laughed, and also raised his glass. 'Who'd have thought it! Great-uncle, your good health, wherever you may be!'

Elisabeth said, 'To my dear guardian ... I owe you everything...'

'Sir William!' said Mr Deeds, and drained his glass.

Elisabeth raised her glass to the portrait, and as she did so, it seemed to her that for a moment the severe features softened, and that Sir William had actually smiled down upon them.

The publishers hope that this book has given you enjoyable reading. Large Print Books are especially designed to be as easy to see and hold as possible. If you wish a complete list of our books please ask at your local library or write directly to:

Dales Large Print Books
Magna House, Long Preston,
Skipton, North Yorkshire.
BD23 4ND

This Large Print Book, for people
who cannot read normal print,
is published under the auspices of

THE ULVERSCROFT FOUNDATION

... we hope you have enjoyed this book.
Please think for a moment about those
who have worse eyesight than you ...
and are unable to even read or enjoy
Large Print without great difficulty.

You can help them by sending a
donation, large or small, to:

**The Ulverscroft Foundation,
1, The Green, Bradgate Road,
Anstey, Leicestershire, LE7 7FU,
England.**
or request a copy of our brochure for
more details.

The Foundation will use all donations
to assist those people who are visually
impaired and need special attention
with medical research, diagnosis
and treatment.

Thank you very much for your help.